I KNOW YOU KILLED THEM

J.A. LEAKE

JACK MCSPORRAN

ALSO BY THE AUTHORS

Co-written Novels

The Girl Who Got Away

Also by J.A. Leake:

The Lies Between Us

Also by Jack McSporran:

Dead Awake

The Maggie Black Series:

- *Vendetta*

- *The Witness*

- *The Defector*

- *Kill Order*

- *Hit List*

- *Payback*

For all my fellow therapists.
- J.A.

For my Auntie Di.
- Jack

1

There are memories that stick with you, no matter how old you get or what happens in your life. Or even when your life completely falls apart. Memories that define who you are.

I remember that I used to play a game with my sister: if you had superpowers, what would they be? She always chose something lame—x-ray vision or super speed. Like, who would that even help? Some pervy guy who liked to spy through locker room walls and then make a speedy getaway?

I always wanted superior mental abilities, like reading people's minds or being telepathic. Professor X was my fave. He didn't even need to walk. He could defeat someone with the strength of his mind alone.

It taught me the mind was a powerful thing.

As it turned out, though, being psychic in the real world just made people think you were crazy.

Maybe super speed and x-ray vision would have been better after all.

"Sadie?" Dr. Williams asked, and I jerked my head up from where I had been pulling a loose thread on the sleeve of my shirt. Dr. Williams watched me with his bushy brows drawn low over his eyes as the light from the floor lamp reflected off his bald head. "Are you still with me?"

I struggled to remember what he'd asked me when I first sat down. I ran my hand along the arm of the threadbare couch in his office as a deep sadness weighed me down. He probably asked what they always do: some variant of, "What brings you here to see me?"

The window behind him revealed a cold, gray sky and bare trees. As if they'd wanted to mimic the bleakness of a winter day, the barren color scheme continued inside with institutional gray walls. The psychiatrist's office had a few pieces of artwork, but even these were uninspiring. Just washed-out water-colors of boring landscapes. I guess he thought we couldn't handle anything more stimulating than that.

I thought of my room at home, everything brightly colored and cheerful. It was like pop art had exploded all over my walls and furniture. In the center of the wall facing my bed, I hung a print of *Mona Cat* by Romero Britto because it made me smile as soon as I woke up. Who doesn't love a brightly colored cat dressed like the Mona Lisa?

Something inside me twisted, and I squeezed my eyes shut tightly against stinging tears. Home.

"Sadie," Dr. Williams said again, his voice a little firmer, "did you hear what I asked?"

I met his gaze. "I don't remember."

"Why do you think you're here?"

I looked out the window again. Just beyond the courtyard with its scrawny trees lay the road that brought me here. Full of potholes, it led to the middle-of-nowhere, Georgia. My house and family were hours away in a suburb outside Atlanta. Thinking of my parents brought a dull ache to my abdomen.

"My parents would rather send me here than listen to me," I said, twisting the hem of my shirt around my finger.

"Your parents?" Dr. Williams repeated idiotically,

like he didn't know what parents were. "And my shrink. He thinks I'm crazy, too," I added, lifting my chin just a tad.

Do you know what delusional means? my old psychiatrist asked me. *It means you believe things to be true that are just fantasy and make believe. Like the comics you love so much.*

"We don't like to use that word here," Dr. Williams said with a little frown.

"What—shrink?"

"No. Crazy. No one here is crazy. Everyone is just dealing with a lot of different stressors. It's my job, along with the other therapists, to help you learn how to manage them appropriately."

I considered him for a moment. That would be nice if it was true. I'd been called that word more times than I could count. By other kids at school, by teachers, and even my own family. I'd never gotten to the point where they locked me in a psych ward before, though.

Not until now.

"I don't want to be here," I said, trying to hide the waver in my voice.

Dr. Williams just watched me, impassive as any other shrink I had cried in front of. They were all immune to tears. "I understand that, Sadie, but you need a facility that can give you constant care."

I wrapped my arms around myself. "How long will I have to be here?"

"That's up to you," he said, leaning back in his chair. "How involved you are in your therapy is the key to getting stable."

I am *stable!* I wanted to scream at him, but I figured it wouldn't go over well. "What kind of therapy?" I asked instead.

"We do a combination of medications, group therapy, and individual therapy here."

I had a sudden urge to escape right then—I hated taking medication. My old psychiatrist always gave me too many, and I ended up feeling like a zombie. At home, my mom didn't monitor it closely. She assumed I took it as prescribed, but I didn't.

I wouldn't get away with that here.

"The first step," he said, pen hovering at the ready above his notepad like I was about to say something profound, "is for you to tell me why you're here."

My hands curled into fists. "Don't you have a file on me? Paperwork that tells you exactly what made them send me here? Why do I have to tell you?"

"It's important that you understand why. That you don't just see it as a punishment."

I leaned forward. "It *is* a punishment," I said through clenched teeth.

"We're going to work on changing that perception," he said in irritatingly patient tones. "For now, just humor me."

Like a sudden wave, a powerful grief crashed over me. I shook my head as tears broke the surface, running down my face like rain. "I don't know."

"You do. You can do this, Sadie."

Images flashed across my mind like lightning:

My sister and I, huddled together in a tent we set up in the living room, reading comics together with a flashlight.

Fire, eagerly consuming the pages of my favorite books.

My sister, screaming.

"Amber," I cried.

Dr. Williams sat up straighter. "Amber, your sister . . . ?" he prompted.

"She's dead." My voice broke. "Because of me."

2

____

I didn't want to remember. I had buried it deep inside me just to hide from it, but Dr. Williams had dragged it to the surface.

He didn't understand that I hadn't just lost my sister. That would have been bad enough.

He didn't know that I was responsible for letting it happen.

My mind splintered and threatened to break apart as the sobs overtook me.

"I know this hurts, Sadie," Dr. Williams said in a surprisingly gentle voice, "but you've done well remembering."

He passed me the box of tissues, but I ignored it. Therapists always did that. They wanted you to stop crying and just move on already, so they handed you some tissues like it could possibly help.

"Sometimes our minds protect us from grief and trauma by making us forget the details. Have you noticed that you've had this problem? Forgetting things?"

I tried to cast my mind back to the night of the fire, but something in my subconscious prevented it. I thought about my parents driving me here. They had shoved me forcibly in the car, literally kicking and screaming. At one point, I had tried the door handle of our SUV. I would have jumped out on the highway just to escape. They had engaged the child lock, though.

We're trying to get you help, Sadie, my mom had said, while my father yelled obscenities. She turned around to look at me, her usually impeccably made-up face looking haggard and drawn. *You haven't been well since Amber died.*

The panic attacks had gotten so bad, I no longer left the house. I hadn't been to school in months. I sat in my room and sketched, or I read comics. Anything else made me completely shut down, unable to move or talk.

When my parents handed me over to the mental health techs here, both had sighed with relief. They wouldn't have to deal with my anxiety and agoraphobia anymore.

I had memories of all these things, but when it came to the details of my sister's death, I couldn't remember much at all.

"There are big blank spots in my memory, especially when it comes to Amber's death," I admitted.

"That can happen with trauma. It could be that your mind isn't ready to face what happened."

"I'll never be ready to face it."

He gave me a look like, *We'll see about that,* and my stomach tightened. "What can you remember about the night your sister died?"

Flames. Screams. The choking smell of smoke.

"No," I said as I expelled the images from my mind. "I don't want to talk about this anymore."

I stood up to leave, and Dr. Williams stood, too. Because of course I couldn't leave. This wasn't a regular therapy visit. My parents trapped me here.

His gaze assessed me, and I knew he was trying to decide if he should call an aid to come restrain me. How he reacted now would show me what I could expect from my time here. Would they come in and hold me down? Give me a shot of something that made me cow-like and docile?

Someone knocked at the door, and I jumped. This was it.

"Just a moment, Sadie," he said, holding up his hand to me like he was trying to calm a wild animal. Wouldn't want to upset the crazy person in the room.

He opened it to reveal a girl about my age, with a slicked-back ponytail, nose piercing, and heavily made-up eyes.

Her gaze flicked to mine briefly before landing on the doctor again. "You asked for me to come by?"

"Yes, Becca, thank you," he said, holding his arm out to usher her into the room. "You're a little early, but this might be better timing."

I stood apart from them, arms wrapped around myself as I surveyed the situation. No mental health techs to give me a shot—that seemed like a good sign—but what was up with the girl? She wore unflattering teal scrubs that made me think she was a patient here, too.

To me, Dr. Williams said, "Sadie, this is Becca. I thought you would rather someone your own age give you a tour of where you'll be staying than some boring old staff member."

"Okay," I said, unable to keep the hesitation

from my voice. I glanced again at her piercings and dark makeup. I thought of all the times I'd attempted to do my own makeup and failed. Amber always made it look easy. She'd watch one video on YouTube, and then she could copy it like a professional. Tears stung my eyes again. Great. Now this girl both reminded me of my dead sister and intimidated me.

"Or would you rather continue our session?" Dr. Williams asked, no doubt picking up on my unease.

I shook my head.

"All right then. If you'll just follow Becca, she'll show you around."

Becca walked out the door without another word, and I followed.

The old wooden floors creaked beneath our footsteps as we walked down the hall away from Dr. Williams's office. I glanced at the ugly puce walls— why did hospitals and institutions always paint walls the same disgusting color?

"So, what's your damage?" Becca asked as we entered the main foyer of the building. Soaring ceilings and a curving staircase made it seem like we'd stepped into some old plantation home. Because that's exactly what this place was—just a big, rambling Southern mansion that had been converted into a psychiatric ward for kids. Badly.

Once, the mansion had been white on the outside with Greco-Roman columns that stretched all the way to the second story. Now it sported dingy, peeling paint. Everything about it seemed to be crumbling. The front porch steps, made of brick, had threatened to give way when I followed the mental health techs into the facility.

I looked longingly back at the front entrance, where two big double doors stood firmly locked. They were heavy, solid wood. No windows to easily break.

I dragged my attention back to Becca. "My parents think I'm crazy."

She eyeballed me. "And you don't?"

"Isn't everyone a little crazy?"

Her laugh echoed in the big open space. "I guess, but not everyone gets locked up in a psych ward, either." She held out her hands expansively as we approached a little office room with an abundance of windows. It sat in the center of the foyer, an island constructed of metal and glass. Inside were rows and rows of pill bottles, like a small pharmacy. A nurse inside the office glanced up from her phone at us briefly before zoning out again. "Which brings us to the focal point of our tour: where you'll line up twice, or maybe even three times a day, like a good sheep and get your meds."

I grimaced. "Great, so they want us all docile and sedated."

She shrugged one shoulder. "It's not so bad—some of them even give you a nice high."

She led me down another short hallway and into what was probably the main living room of the house at one time. Tables and chairs had been set up so it resembled a nursing home's activity center, only instead of Bingo, a bunch of kids in scrubs sat around talking to each other, playing cards, or just staring into space. The enormous fireplace on one side of the room had been walled off, and none of the windows had curtains, so it still managed to maintain its institutional feel.

Before we could walk into the room, a girl pushed past us, mumbling to herself. I glanced at her bald head in surprise. At first I thought she had cancer, but then I saw all the nicks and stubbly black hair. She'd done it to herself.

"Don't mind her," Becca said with a shake of her head. "She did a Britney circa 2007 the other day."

We continued down the hall, the smell of food wafting in the air. It had that overpowering cafeteria scent to it, like whatever it was had a ton of onions in it.

I hated onions.

When we came to a dim back staircase, Becca pointed up. "That's where all the rooms are. There's an elevator off the entryway, but it's faster to take the stairs." She started up them before saying over her shoulder, "Also, the elevator smells like shit ever since one of the schizo kids smeared it on the walls."

I gripped the handrail tighter. This had to be a nightmare I was having. Surely I'd wake up, and I'd be safe in my bed at home. The glow in the dark stars my parents had stuck to my ceiling when I was four would shine down on me. I didn't belong here. I wasn't some schizo who smeared shit on the walls.

My chest tightened, and by the time I reached the top of the stairs, I panted for breath. Becca watched me as my throat tightened.

"I get those, too," she said quietly. "Panic attack, right?"

I nodded, unable to speak.

"It gets better. Being here. I mean, at first it feels like someone locked you up and threw away the key, but then you get used to it. Some of the groups aren't bad—like art therapy. No way in hell my mom would ever pay for art classes for me, so I figure this is the next best thing."

At some point during Becca's short monologue, my chest and throat had loosened just enough that I could speak again.

"Thanks," I said weakly.

She shrugged it off and continued down the hall. "This one's yours," she said, pointing to a plain white door on the left side.

A small dry erase board had been attached to the front of the door, and the names Millie and Lisa were written there. Before I could ask who they were, the door opened, and a small girl with mousy brown hair just barely squeezed through.

She didn't meet my eyes as she pushed her over-sized glasses higher on her nose. She looked about ten years old.

"This is your roommate, Millie," Becca said and reached out to ruffle her hair.

Millie flashed a ghost of a smile before hurrying off down the hall to the staircase.

"You like peace and quiet?" Becca asked.

"I guess?"

"You'll love having Millie as a roommate, then. She has selective mutism. She hasn't spoken a word in years."

It hit me again, that sense that I was in the wrong place. Sure, I had anxiety and panic attacks, but I didn't choose to be *mute.* "How old is she? She doesn't look old enough to be here."

"She's thirteen, so she just made the cutoff."

It could be worse, I guessed. I could have had the shaved head girl for a roomie. She looked like she was dealing with something intense.

And might shave my head in the night, too.

Becca opened the door for me, and I stepped inside. My mood plummeted like a broken elevator. The institutional theme continued into the room, with furniture that had plain white blankets and pillows. The beige walls—an improvement over puce?—featured a distinctive lack of windows or mirrors. They must have feared we'd break the glass and cut ourselves. One of the beds had a single threadbare stuffed dog, so it must have been Millie's.

Instead of a closet, our clothes would be stored in two dressers that sat against either wall. There were also two small desks with chairs, though I didn't know what those were for. None of us had homework thanks to being on forced medical leave, and they didn't let us have our phones, much less laptops.

When I first got here, they made me hand over all my stuff, like a prisoner. They had big white bags marked *Patient Belongings*, and everything I owned went into them. Then they labeled the bags and locked them away in a storeroom.

I had nothing to make the room more comfortable. No pillows or blankets from home. No brightly colored artwork to provide something else to look at besides these boring ass walls.

Not even a phone to distract myself with.

"I don't think I can sleep here," I said to Becca, who smirked.

"Nightmarish, right? It doesn't have to look this plain, though—you're allowed to hang pictures and stuff. Millie just likes it like that. I mean, I guess she does. She never says differently."

"Where's the bathroom?" I asked, my stomach threatening to toss what little I'd eaten that morning.

Becca gestured for me to follow her out of the room before pointing down the hall. "Second door on your right."

I managed to make it to the sink before splashing vomit everywhere.

I found out pretty fast that psych wards do not like you losing your shit in the bathroom. It was the mirror that triggered it. After I rinsed my mouth, I'd glanced up to look at my reflection and saw only a garbled distortion. My normally reddish-blond hair looked dull and brown, while my eyes were wide with fear. Instead of a normal mirror, a piece of shiny metal hung on the wall. For me, it just hammered home that I was officially locked up in an insane asylum.

I only remember pieces of what happened after that. The screaming. Me trying to rip the "mirror" off the wall. Becca reaching for me, trying to calm me down. I clenched my teeth at the memory of shoving her. She'd called for help after that.

Now, I glanced around me in the dark and felt around with my hands. Scratchy blankets and sheets. Flimsy pillow. So at some point, I'd gone to bed. Either that, or they'd put me there. From the other side of the room came a soft snore, and I could just make out a small form huddled under blankets in the dim glow of a nightlight.

I tried to sit up. A terrible weight held me down,

like each of my limbs weighed a ton. My head swam, and my vision blurred. A sedative. They'd drugged me—probably given me a shot while I was shouting like a maniac in the bathroom.

Tears pricked my eyes. They may not have put my hands and legs in physical restraints, but I'd been restrained, nonetheless. I tried to roll over on my side, but I couldn't even do that. The drug still coursing through my veins threatened to pull me under again, like a riptide I couldn't fight.

Against my will, my eyelids closed. Total darkness. My mind started to slip away, even as I struggled to hold on.

And then a sound pierced the stillness of my room: a hair-raising scream.

I fought to open my eyes. Where had that come from? Through my sluggish consciousness, I tried to analyze the noise. Definitely a scream, like someone had been attacked. And close—down the hall, maybe?

I strained my ears, but I could only hear Millie's soft breathing. The scream hadn't woken her, then.

The drug pulled me down harder, more insistently, and for a moment, I succumbed to it.

The scream came again, so loud and agonizing

that it penetrated even my forced unconsciousness. But I couldn't fight it. Someone was screaming outside my room, and I couldn't even open my eyes again.

What the hell was this place?

3

I woke in the morning to the sound of faint rustling. Without windows, the room lacked the natural light to tell me what time it was, but enough light came under the door to at least see around me. Beside her bed, Millie got dressed in the same unflattering teal scrubs I'd seen everyone else wear. The rustling sound came from her making her bed.

"Hi," I said with a tentative smile.

She turned and gave a little wave.

"This is kind of awkward since we already slept in the same room, but I'm Sadie." She nodded, but didn't try to introduce herself. I wondered how she communicated—did she just use body language, or did she have some sort of writing device to convey her thoughts? Either way, I couldn't imagine a more frustrating existence. Whatever happened to make her like that must have been fucked up in the extreme.

I glanced around the barren room. "Are we supposed to go somewhere now?" My stomach grumbled, and I put a hand over it to cover the noise. "Breakfast, maybe?"

She nodded again and beckoned with one hand. When I stood up out of bed, I noticed two things: one, dizziness hit me so powerfully I almost had to sit back down again, and two, I now wore ugly teal scrubs just like Millie's.

"Where are my clothes?" I asked, my voice coming out both sharp and high-pitched. Millie shot me a sympathetic look. "They drugged me, stripped me, and put me in these ugly scrubs?"

No further sympathetic looks came from Millie, so I had to assume this was the type of treatment I could expect here.

"That's just great," I muttered. "Did they at least give me a toothbrush and toothpaste?"

She nodded and pointed toward the door.

"Will you wait for me while I brush my teeth and use the bathroom, then?"

When it seemed like she'd stick around, I slipped

out the door and headed for the bathroom. It surprised me to find that the hall was empty—I'd half-expected to be under some sort of guard after yesterday's breakdown. But they must have thought the drugging effects of the shot they gave me would keep me docile.

The bathroom had old-fashioned white tile shaped like a honeycomb. A row of five simple white sinks hung on the wall, with the metal mirrors above them. Two girls brushed their teeth at the sinks, but they didn't turn to look at me when I walked by. Aside from the five bathroom stalls, a row of curtains revealed four dingy-looking showers. Up against one wall, a cabinet stood with its doors open. Supplies sat neatly lined up on the shelves inside: toothbrushes, toothpaste, period supplies, shampoo, conditioner, soap, towels. I noticed that anything remotely sharp was missing. No razors or handheld mirrors.

I grabbed a toothbrush and a little tube of toothpaste. The other two girls had left while I was in the stall, neither of them ever saying a word. I turned my back on the metal mirrors while I brushed, focusing on the showers instead. I would have to come back later and take one, but I didn't want to keep Millie waiting.

My scrubs made an annoying swishing sound

with every movement I made. Another wave of dizziness hit me, and I wondered again what horrible drug they'd given me.

A little bubble of panic rose at the thought, and my hands shook.

I didn't belong here. At the same time, I knew my parents wouldn't let me come home yet. Not unless I could convince the doctor nothing was wrong with me. And my freak-out in the bathroom hadn't helped anything.

For now, I was trapped.

W hen I came out of the bathroom, I let out my breath in relief. Millie stood against the wall, staring down at the floor. Becca had shown me around before, but I really didn't want to have to wander these halls alone, trying to find wherever we were supposed to go in the morning.

"Thanks for waiting," I said, and she shrugged in answer.

She headed toward the stairs, shoulders hunched and head down, like she didn't want anyone to notice her. I followed, and when we got to the big main entrance to the psych ward, she led me to the glass-encased room that looked like a mini pharmacy. A whole line of kids stood waiting in front of it, singing something and clapping rhythmically—like a bus song when you're off to summer camp.

When I got closer, I could hear the words: "If you're happy and you know it, shake your pills." A bored-looking nurse handed each kid who came to the window two small cups and watched as they downed first one and then the other. I grimaced. The last thing I wanted was more medicine coursing through my veins.

I glanced at the nearby hallway—would they even notice if I slipped out of line and went that way?

"I wouldn't if I were you," a voice said from behind me. I turned to find Becca shaking her head at me. "Not after that stunt you pulled yesterday. They'll put you in isolation for sure."

I stared at her for a moment, trying to figure out how she read my mind. But then I realized I had already drifted out of the line and inched toward the hallway. "Breakfast better be good if I have to put up with this first."

She laughed. "Oh don't worry, it's not."

"Great," I muttered.

"But basically, taking those pills first is the only way you're not going to starve to death here."

"Wow. That's not abusive at all."

With a shrug, she gently steered me back in line. "The quickest way out of here is to do what they want."

I glanced back at her. "What's it like being in a cult?"

She snorted. "Girl, shut up."

We waited in line while everyone around me continued to sing their happy pill song. Millie stood a few kids away in the queue, keeping her head down and avoiding any contact with anyone else. She quickly and quietly took her meds before hurrying down the hall. Watching her made my heart ache.

When it was my turn, the dead-eyed nurse asked for my name and birthdate. After I told her, she handed me two tiny paper cups, one with three different pills, and one with water.

Becca leaned to look at the pills over my shoulder. "Nice. The blue ones make you mellow as smoking pot."

"Swallow the pills with the water and hand both cups back to me," the nurse said, her tone of voice as monotonous as a robot's.

"What are these?" I asked, shaking the cup at her.

Her eyes narrowed. "Whatever Dr. Williams prescribed."

"You don't know what they are?"

Becca pulled me aside. With quick, stabbing motions, she pointed at the pills. "Anti-anxiety, mood stabilizer, antidepressant. Just take them, okay? Before she pushes the button and calls them to give you something a little stronger."

I looked up to find the nurse giving me a hard stare. "Take the pills where I can see you," she said.

I nearly flung my hands up in frustration, but then I remembered the cup of pills and water. They would be seriously pissed if I scattered the medicine all over the floor. With a frown, I tossed each one back, one after the other. Crumpling the paper cups, I handed them to the nurse.

I stood to the side, arms folded over my chest while Becca downed her pills, too.

"Breakfast time," she said, pulling me down the same hall Millie had disappeared into.

The smell of eggs and pancakes hit me as soon as we walked into the dining room. It made my stomach growl until I got a look at the closest plate— the eggs had a brownish tint to them like they'd been cooked in old grease, and the pancakes looked completely flat. At least there were glasses of juice.

Kids sat around tables, but unlike the scene at a school cafeteria, hardly anyone laughed or joked around. Almost everyone looked half-asleep—thanks to the meds we'd all been forced to take just now, I supposed.

Becca led me to a window where the kitchen served up the unappealing eggs and pancakes on trays. They threw in a couple packs of margarine and syrup, and I noticed the utensils were the flimsiest type of plastic—the kind that will snap if you so much as breathe on it wrong.

After getting her tray, Becca walked to a nearby round table and sat with two other kids who were nearly finished eating. I stood there for a moment awkwardly, unsure if she wanted me to join them or not. When she didn't glance my way, I took a deep breath and sat down at their table. I hated social stuff like this. I always second guessed everything I said and did.

Becca smiled at me around a mouthful of food, and my shoulders relaxed. "Sadie, this is Danny and Katelyn."

They both waved at me. Danny had an impressive number of piercings—nose, eyebrows, lip, and multiple ones on both ears. Rail-thin with sky-blue hair, he reminded me of an anime character.

"Who'd you get for a roommate?" Katelyn asked, her dark brown eyes warm and friendly. With her jet-black hair, rounded, open face, distinctive lack of piercings, and curvier body, she looked like Danny's opposite.

"Millie," I said, and she and Becca shared a look I didn't understand. "What?"

"That room's just seen some stuff, is all," Katelyn said with a wave of her hand.

"Like with previous roommates or something?"

Becca nodded. "Millie's last roommate was always freaking out."

That reminded me of the screams I heard the night before. I still wasn't sure if I'd dreamed them or not. "Was anyone freaking out last night?"

They all gave me curious looks. "What do you mean?" Danny asked, arms crossed on the table now like he'd completely given up trying to eat the sad breakfast on his plate.

"I thought I heard screaming."

Danny shrugged. "I wouldn't know. I take so many different sleep meds that a literal hurricane wouldn't wake me up."

Becca smirked and took a sip of her water. "I

mean, *you* freaked out on me. I had to call a tech to come inject your ass." She put her cup back down. "Sorry about that, by the way."

The sedative kept my reactions dulled, but a little twinge of embarrassment made it through. "I guess you think I'm totally batshit crazy now."

Becca held up her thumb and pointer finger a short distance from each other. "Only a little."

"'We're all mad here,'" Danny quoted with a grin.

"Anyway, other than you screaming earlier, I didn't hear anything. I'm all the way down the hall from you, though," Becca said.

"I'm a few doors down," Katelyn said with a furrow in the middle of her brows. "But I didn't hear screaming. When you've been here a while, though, you learn to block stuff out at night."

"Maybe I just imagined it then," I said, though I didn't think so. It seemed so real. I could still hear the echo of those piercing screams reverberating in my mind. The hair on the back of my neck stood up, and I rubbed my hand over it.

"There's no denying you had a hard night," Katelyn said with a laugh. "No offense, girl, but you look rough."

"Katelyn," Danny said in a mock-scolding voice, "rude."

"I'm sorry I didn't have a chance to do my hair and makeup this morning—in this insane asylum," I snapped.

Katelyn held up her hands with a grin. "Sorry, sorry. Sometimes I say things without thinking. It's one of my issues."

Using your mental illness as an excuse to say mean things sounded like just being a shitty person to me, but I decided not to make a big deal out of it. We were all going through stuff here. Who knew what Katelyn's story was.

Becca and Katelyn continued eating, but I couldn't really stomach more of the rubbery eggs and freezer-burnt pancakes. I let my gaze wander around the room.

As if pulled by a magnet, it landed on a guy sitting near the entrance. Our eyes locked, and I realized he'd been staring at me. That was what drew my gaze. Heat flooded my cheeks because, to be honest, we may have been in a psych ward, but he looked like a model. Dark, messy hair, chiseled jaw and cheekbones, and full lips that I could see even from across the room.

The moment he looked away, I gently elbowed

Becca. "Hey," I said, keeping my voice low. "Who is that?"

Becca glanced where I'd nodded with my chin and sighed. "That's Aaron. But look, you need to stay away from him, okay? Just trust me on that."

I looked at the others, but they just nodded in agreement. "Oh, come on, you gotta give me more than that," I said.

Before anyone could answer me, a loud gagging sound interrupted us. The same girl I saw the day before, the one with the badly shaved head, got up so fast from her table that her chair fell with a clatter. She spat her food out in a disgusting wad on her plate. "Don't eat the eggs!" she screamed, her eyes bulging. "They're poisoned! They're trying to kill us!"

Everyone stopped what they were doing to watch her, but no one seemed panicked that they'd suddenly keel over from breakfast. Still, I let my fork drop to my plate.

Our lack of reaction only made her face redder. When no one immediately started throwing away their food, she stomped to the nearest table and grabbed up another girl's tray. Before the kid could do anything to stop her, she hurled the tray and all its messy contents toward the nearest wall.

Two of the mental health techs hurried out of the room, and Becca shook her head. "This isn't going to be good."

I couldn't look away.

Letting out a guttural scream, the girl continued snatching up trays and hurling them at the wall. Before she could grab another, two of the biggest techs came on either side of her and held onto her arms.

She fought them like an alligator, rolling and screeching and trying to wrench away. It took another two men to restrain her. A fifth came with a needle. With gloved hands, he inserted it in her upper arm, while the others struggled to hold her still. My heart pounded and the disgusting eggs I'd eaten threatened to come back up. Was this what I looked like in the bathroom last night?

A few more moments of fighting, and she suddenly went limp. I watched in silent horror as they hauled her out of the room.

I glanced over at Becca, but she just calmly drank her juice. When she finished, she stood up and grabbed her tray. "Time for group—you coming?"

All around, others were doing the same, so I slowly got to my feet.

Apparently, some girl losing her mind and getting

hauled out of here like a tranquilized bear was no big deal.

If you weren't already nuts when you came in here, then watching stuff like this on a regular basis would help you reach that level in a hurry.

4

Twelve of us sat in mismatched chairs in a loose circle, and I tried not to stare awkwardly at the girl across from me. She kept picking at a spot on her arm to the point that it started bleeding. Once it did, she let the blood flow enough to draw patterns with it on her skin. I shuddered and tried to look at something else.

The room consisted almost entirely of windows, including part of the ceiling, like it had been a sunroom or greenhouse or something at one point. Condensation formed on the outside of the glass, each bead of water tracing down the window in a hypnotically meandering trail. The garden outside looked neglected, with spindly, bare trees and an abundance of dead vegetation. An empty fountain stood in the middle of a cracked concrete patio, its cherub statue forlorn and abandoned. It seemed to fit the colorless insides of this place.

Becca and Katelyn chatted beside me, but their words flitted past my ears meaninglessly as my gaze wandered the room. Again, I had that sensation that someone watched me. I turned my head to see Aaron sitting across from me—near the skin picker. Our gazes caught and held for a moment before he shifted to something else. Maybe it should have been creepy to draw the attention of someone in a mental facility, but Aaron didn't give off crazy vibes. Something about him made me feel calm.

A woman breezed in, interrupting my thoughts. Instead of scrubs or a white coat, she wore a brightly patterned long skirt, oversized sweater, and what seemed like ten jangling bracelets on each wrist. Her frizzy hair, shot with gray, floated in an untamed cloud around her shoulders.

"Hello everyone," she said in a surprisingly girlish voice. "Most of you are old friends and have participated in my group before. Still, I like to introduce myself each time for those of us who find it difficult to keep names in our heads. I'm Dr. Mendez, but you must all call me Julia because when we're in this circle together, we're all equals."

I scoffed quietly at that. *Yeah, except for the fact that you can walk out of group and leave this place anytime you want.*

"Let's start with the usual," she said with a jingle of bracelets. "We'll go around and check in with each other on how we're feeling emotionally, mentally, physically, and spiritually. I'll start just to give all of you a refresher."

She closed her eyes. "Physically, my back's been twinging a bit, so I'll have to be careful not to throw it out. Emotionally, I'm feeling pretty joyful, even though mentally my thoughts have been scattered today," she added with a little shake of her head. "And spiritually, I'm feeling connected."

I dropped my gaze to the floor when she opened her eyes again. I couldn't even tell myself how I felt right now, much less convey it to the group. This better not be one of those forced-participation situations. I broke out in hives anytime I even heard the words "ice breaker."

"Who's next?" she asked, and to my surprise, three people raised their hands. "Let's see. How about you go first, Jon?"

She nodded toward a boy sitting to the right of Aaron. He looked like he'd been cast as Aaron's physical opposite, so pale he looked like he'd been bleached all over by the sun. He ran a hand through white-blonde hair before popping his neck.

"Physically, my stomach hurts after eating that shitty breakfast. Emotionally, I feel as pissed off as I always do. Mentally, all I can think about is getting out of here, and spiritually, I feel disconnected because there is no God."

I thought the counselor would reprimand him for his language and possibly even his negative attitude, but all she said was, "Thank you for sharing. Let's keep going around the circle."

I only half-listened to everyone's responses after that. I kept rehearsing in my head what I'd say when it was my turn, while gripping the seat of my chair hard enough to turn my knuckles white. I kept hoping someone else would say they didn't want to speak, but the only one Julia skipped over was Millie. Was it too late to claim I had selective mutism?

Suddenly, everyone's attention was on me. I glanced over at Becca, and she nodded encouragingly. "Um," I said, and my voice immediately cracked. My cheeks flushed as I cleared my throat. "I feel groggy, anxious, and my thoughts are slower than normal. Spiritually, I guess I feel disconnected —it's hard to feel very spiritual in a place like this."

Some murmurs of agreement went around the

circle as I let out my breath in a rush and leaned back in my chair.

"Thank you for being so brave," Julia said with a serene smile. "This next part will be a little more intense, though, so I ask that you only share with the group if you feel comfortable." I inwardly shook my head. No way was I talking about my past again, but at least she was giving us the chance to stay silent this time.

"I would like for you to tell us your story. What brought you here and what you've been working through. Even if you've told us before, you never know how much it could help someone else. Someone who's going through something similar, or maybe just knowing you're not alone in dealing with some pretty hard stuff."

A silence filled the room except for the occasional shifting of a chair or sniffle. I didn't have to look up to know Aaron still watched me. I could feel his eyes. Well, if he was waiting to hear why I was here, he'd be waiting a long time.

Becca sighed loudly beside me and sat up straighter. "Fine. I'll go."

"Thank you, Becca," Julia said.

"Short version: I took two handfuls of pills and tried to kill myself." She waved one hand over the length of her body. "Obviously, I didn't do it right."

I caught a lot of sympathetic nods from the group. These were kids who knew the siren call of suicide—myself included.

Julia shifted in a light jingling of bracelets before giving Becca a penetrating look. "And the long version?"

Becca seemed to shrink into herself. She hugged her knees to her chest as she curled up in the chair. "Can I just tell parts of it?"

"Of course. Whatever makes you most comfortable," Julia said.

Becca fixed her gaze on the window across from her. "My mom's the one who found me and got me to the hospital right away. Turns out, pills aren't especially effective if they can catch it fast enough to pump your stomach. And it just so happens she came home early that day. If it had been my stepdad, he could have stumbled over my unconscious body and not given a shit." She scoffed, but it lacked venom. "Not that my mom gives much of a shit, but at least she wouldn't just ignore me if I was dying."

I thought of my own mom, who had always loved my sister best. She wouldn't step over my unconscious body either, but she'd also rather send me off for help than do anything about it herself.

"That sounds like a difficult environment to live in," Julia said.

Becca whipped her head toward Julia. "Difficult? That's like having a mom or dad who yells a lot. How about a stepdad that puts cigarettes out on your thighs? Or a mom that just leaves the room when he gets out the baseball bat he likes to beat me with." Her face darkened. "But all of that is nothing compared to what happens at night."

She didn't have to say anything else. We all knew what she meant. I could tell from the way the girls suddenly wrapped their arms protectively around themselves or the way the boys shifted uncomfortably.

Deep inside me, something stirred in reaction to that, a memory struggling to come to the surface. I immediately shoved the thought away and focused on my breathing.

"I have a caseworker, but she's more interested in her own life, I guess. She hasn't done much to help. I kept getting deeper in that black hole of depression, and I started thinking I'd be better off dead. Now I'm here. It's better than home."

Throughout her story, Becca's voice stayed level,

as though she'd told it a hundred times and it no longer affected her. But I watched her now as she straightened an invisible wrinkle in her scrub top. Her hands shook.

Julia jumped in with feedback, but I couldn't concentrate on what she was saying.

Becca hadn't given many details, but my mind suddenly became crowded with horrifying images, as though she had. As I focused on the calming trails of condensation on the windows, I caught Aaron watching me again. His expression looked concerned, like he could tell my mind was torturing me.

Another voice drew my attention away from Aaron. Katelyn, who sat on the other side of Becca, brushed her hair out of her eyes and said, "I know what you mean about this place being better than home. I don't want to go back."

Julia made a humming sound in her throat. "You feel safe here?"

Katelyn nodded. "I like knowing what to expect."

"Routines can offer that stability we need when everything else in our life feels like it's falling apart."

"Yeah, and I made friends here," Katelyn said.

Her voice sounded strained, like she was holding back tears. "I don't have many friends at home."

"Then let's talk about some ways you can prepare yourself to leave, Katelyn. And I'm sure others will have some suggestions for you, too. Why don't you start by telling us some of the things you worry about when you think about going home?"

"I'm afraid I'll start cutting again, especially when I get back and remember my mom won't be there anymore." Her voice broke, and an answering grief rose within me. I tried to push it away, but it clung to me like the smell of smoke. My throat burned as, just for a moment, my sister's face flashed in my mind.

Katelyn kept talking through her tears, and a cold feeling washed over me. It felt like being plunged in ice cold water, with every fine hair on my neck standing on end. At the same time, I broke out in a cold sweat. I had to rub my palms on my pant legs to dry them.

"Grief is one of the hardest emotions to go through," Julia said sympathetically. "And it would be a lie to say going home won't be a huge trigger for you. Because you're right, when you get there, and your mom isn't there, it's going to be really hard. But what are some ways we've talked about that will help you manage those emotions?"

Katelyn thought for a moment. "Journaling has helped. Maybe taking my dog for a walk? My mom always liked doing that."

"I am so proud of you, Katelyn," Julia said, gently slapping her own knee for emphasis. "Those are both great ways to process your grief in a healthy way. Journaling can help you put those thoughts and emotions down on paper so you can understand exactly how you're feeling. You can even use your journal to write a letter to your mom to help you remember her.

"Walking your dog is also great because you get outside, get some exercise, which helps you physically and emotionally. It sounds like it's also a way to feel close to your mom, since it's an activity she used to enjoy doing."

Katelyn smiled at Julia through her tears. "My dad and grandparents will be there to help me, too. My grandma is a lot like my mom, so that helps."

I could picture everything Katelyn said, like I was watching a reality show on Netflix or something. I saw her getting home, crying because her mom wasn't there to greet her. Being surrounded by family members who loved her, and throwing her arms around a big, fluffy dog.

The uncomfortable feeling washed over me again, like suddenly coming down with the flu. But I knew I wasn't sick.

This wasn't the first time I'd felt this way.

It happened before Amber died.

Nausea reared up so violently I had to press my hand to my mouth. I didn't dare get up and draw attention to myself, so I just tried to breathe slowly through my nose as tears filled my eyes.

An image appeared in my mind, impossible to ignore:

Katelyn, her inky-black hair spread out over her pillows as she lay in her bed, eyes unseeing.

A whisper ran through my mind then. The same thing I'd heard when I lost my sister.

Katelyn is going to die.

5

———

I lost track of time. Julia ended the group, but I couldn't move. The terrible image of Katelyn lying dead in her room kept replaying through my head like a horror film. Other kids got up and started leaving the room, but I stayed glued to my chair. How would it happen? Overdose? Some kind of weird health problem she had that no one knew about?

I thought of something I saw online once about a teenager dying from a freak brain aneurism. She told her parents she had a headache and went to sleep. She never woke up again.

The night before Amber died, I had this terrible flu-like feeling before bed. That night, I dreamed of the fire. Would I dream about Katelyn's death tonight? How would I ever go to sleep?

My breathing became more and more labored, like an elephant had sat on top of my chest. At the same time, my heart beat like I had just sprinted two miles.

Out of the corner of my eye, I saw Becca bend down to my ear. "Do you need help?"

I hesitated for a moment before nodding. I wouldn't normally let someone help me, but I didn't want Julia to notice and call the mental health techs to give me another shot.

She took one arm, and Katelyn took the other. I jerked at Katelyn's touch like it shocked me. I felt responsible for what I'd seen, but how could I possibly warn her of something like that? What if I was wrong? Then they'd all think I deserved to be here.

"Let's go to the bathroom," Becca said, and they gently tugged me in that direction.

We passed Millie on our way out of the group room, her expression twisted in concern. She fell in behind us, as silently as a shadow.

Becca pushed open the door with her shoulder and led me into the downstairs restroom, the eye-watering scent of strong disinfectant burning my nostrils. They let me go, and Katelyn's face filled with concern.

My breaths came in shallow pants as my lungs constricted. I shook like I was freezing cold, but beads of sweat dotted my hairline. Soon, little white dots filled my vision while the edges darkened.

Becca pushed on my shoulder. "Sit down with your head between your legs and take deep breaths."

I did as she said, but every time I breathed through my nose, the chemical smell of fake lemons made my head spin. Instead, I took huge open-mouthed breaths, like a fish flopping on land.

I couldn't look at Katelyn. Every time I did, my stomach threatened to empty on the floor. Millie kneeled beside me and started stroking my hair soothingly. I glanced over at her, surprised.

"Smoke?" Becca offered, holding a cigarette out. I shook my head. "It might help calm your nerves." When I still didn't take it, she moved toward the window and opened it enough to smoke out of. Cold air rushed in.

"You gotta be careful freaking out like that in group," Katelyn said, but I didn't look up. "They'll haul you to Dr. Williams, and then he'll spend hours grilling you, pretending he's doing therapy."

"Yeah," Becca said with a scoff. "And then when

he makes zero progress because he sucks so bad at counseling, he'll just call in a tech to give you a shot."

"I know, right?" Katelyn said. "He's supposed to be this super famous psychiatrist who can help the worst cases, but obviously whoever decided that hasn't been in therapy with him." I could feel her eyes on me as she shifted her attention. "What triggered your panic attack, anyway?"

Again, I saw Katelyn lying dead in her room, and I squeezed my eyes shut so tightly it almost hurt.

"You don't need to answer that," Becca said. "We aren't shrinks."

"I'm just saying, sometimes it helps to talk about what scared you," Katelyn said. I could hear the bristle in her tone at Becca's scolding. "We can probably even help. We've been through some shit, too."

"Don't go all Dr. Williams on us now," Becca said as I struggled to get my breathing under control. "All you need to do is start asking about her childhood, and you'll sound just like him."

Katelyn said something else, but I tried to just focus on Millie's light touch on my hair, which was strangely hypnotic. Usually I couldn't stand to be touched, especially when I was freaking out. But her hand kept bringing me back to the present moment instead of getting lost in my head.

Still, I couldn't stop thinking about the last time I'd felt that way. Like déjà vu on steroids. The night before my sister died, I saw her burn in a fire. And now I saw Katelyn dead, too.

It had to be a mistake. How could anyone die in this place? With its metal mirrors and plastic utensils? With staff ready to drug you into oblivion at the first sign of you freaking out? Unless she really had some kind of strange medical condition. And what were the chances of that?

Little by little, I convinced myself it had all been in my mind. I *did* have a penchant for horror flicks.

"My last session with him, he wanted me to go back to when I was a fucking preschooler," Becca was saying as I slowly regained control over my emotions.

Katelyn laughed, and I managed to look at her without my muscles tensing. She leaned against the nearest sink, looking genuinely entertained by their conversation. She didn't look like someone who was suicidal or was about to die.

"Preschool?" Katelyn asked. "How can you remember preschool?"

"You can't! So I made shit up. I told him I remembered the teacher telling me I was stupid because I couldn't read and that the other kids bullied me. He ate it up. Said all of that contributed to my crappy self-esteem because I kept hearing the preschool teacher telling me I was an idiot."

Katelyn snorted out a laugh. "He's the idiot for believing that."

Becca glanced over when she saw me coming out of my squatting position. "Better now?"

I shot her a weak smile. "Better. Thank you."

She stubbed out her cigarette and tossed it through the window. "Of course. We look out for our own here."

I turned to thank Millie, too, but then I saw she'd somehow slipped out the door already.

"Millie hates to be thanked," Katelyn said with a quick eye roll. "One of her many quirks."

"Now that you've recovered," Becca said with a nod toward the door. "We better go make an appearance in the common room before they notice we're gone."

She went through the door first, and Katelyn followed.

As Katelyn brushed past my arm, her hand was ice cold. Like she was dead already.

A shudder ran down my spine.

I tried not to think about what I'd seen, and by the time we were supposed to report to the dining room again for lunch, I'd locked the thoughts so tightly away in my mind that I could act halfway normal again. We stood in line for something that smelled suspiciously like meatloaf and mashed potatoes. The thought of choking that down almost made me gag, but I resisted the urge. I knew from experience that not eating while taking all these meds only made their effects worse. I'd be a groggy, empty-headed mess for sure.

Katelyn and Becca were in front of me, talking about some show I had never seen. A dystopian where a bunch of kids who have been orbiting the earth have to return and save it somehow. I didn't really see the point in talking about shows we couldn't watch here. It only made me miss my phone and laptop.

Just as I was about to ask them if we at least had access to some books around here, I sensed someone join the line behind me and subtly clear his throat.

I turned and locked eyes with the boy who'd been watching me all day.

"Hi," he said, his smile as warm as his voice. "I'm Aaron."

"I know," I said, and he raised an eyebrow.

"You do?"

I nodded toward Katelyn and Becca. "Yeah, my friends told me."

He grinned. "And here I was thinking maybe I was some sort of celebrity. Although being well known around this place might not be an accomplishment."

I smiled back at him. "Yeah, I think here it's less famous and more infamous."

"Exactly," he said with a laugh.

"I'm Sadie, by the way," I added, tucking my hair behind my ear.

"And you just got here?"

I nodded. "Yesterday."

"Been pretty hard, huh? Adjusting to being here, I mean."

I thought of panicking in the bathroom and waking up medicated. "Was it that obvious?"

"I just know it was hard for me, and then I could tell group triggered you. Sorry if I was staring," he added with a sheepish look.

Warmth creeped up my neck. Knowing he had seen me freaking out during group made me want to hide in my room the rest of the day.

"It gets better," he added. "I almost don't hate it here now."

"How long have you been here?"

"Two months."

I had to bite down to keep my mouth from falling open. Hell if I was going to be locked up here that long!

"You definitely know what you're talking about then," I said, to hide my shock. I wondered how long Becca had been here. I wouldn't be surprised if Millie had been here for months, but it was hard to picture the same for Becca and Katelyn. They seemed almost . . . normal.

He opened his mouth to say something else, but then suddenly the lunch lady waved a tray at me.

"Guess it's my turn for meatloaf," I said with a grimace, and he chuckled.

The lunch lady served the grayish meat topped with bright red sauce, chalky looking potatoes, and peas. As soon as my tray was full, Becca tugged on my arm.

"Come sit with us," she said.

I turned back to say something to Aaron, but she tugged more insistently. The lunch lady was barking orders at him, so it kept him distracted. Still, I didn't understand what Becca's problem was.

The minute we got to the table where Danny and Katelyn waited, I glared at her. "Why are you so anti-Aaron?"

"He's just no good for you to be talking to," Becca said, and the others nodded in agreement.

"Okay, you're going to have to give me more than that. Is he secretly a psycho or something?"

Danny laughed. "No more than the rest of us."

"Then what? He has a girlfriend or something?"

"He used to go out with Lisa," Katelyn said with a mouth full of food.

Becca immediately gave her a look. "Shut up."

I thought of the name beside Millie's on my door, and how the last time I asked about her, I'd been ignored. "Who's Lisa?"

"I really don't like these questions," Danny said with a wave of his hand. "May I be excused?"

"She's gone now," Katelyn said, like that would explain anything.

"She got released?" I asked.

Danny started to get up from the table with a huff, but Becca made him sit back down.

"Not exactly," Katelyn hedged.

They all acted so cagey it made me want to scream. "Then what do you mean by *gone*?"

Katelyn and Becca shared a long look. "We're not supposed to talk about it."

Frustration rose inside me so violently it made my eyes water. "You guys. Seriously. You're being super sketchy right now."

Danny heaved another sigh and reached for my hand. "I know, and we hate being like this, trust me. But it's for your own good. You don't want to know all the details."

"Okay," I said slowly. "But then what does this person who's sort of gone but you can't explain the details have to do with Aaron?"

Becca leveled me with her gaze. "Aaron has a type of girl he attaches himself to, and you're like the perfect match—you get me? It didn't work out between him and Lisa, so we just don't want to see you getting hurt."

I let out my breath. "For fuck's sake, why didn't you say that from the beginning? That sounds much more reasonable and less creepy than whatever you guys were implying before."

Danny laughed and did a one-shouldered shrug. "We can't help if we're dramatic!"

Katelyn and Becca laughed, too, but I didn't miss the look of relief they shared.

6

After lunch, Cathy, one of the techs, told us to line up for recreation. She kept checking her phone like she'd rather be anywhere but with us. I queued up with Becca, Danny, and Katelyn. Millie, Aaron, and some other kids brought up the rear as we followed Cathy to one of the rear entrances. Before we went outside, she handed us each a thin jacket. Luckily, we lived in Georgia where the weather stayed pretty mild, even in January. Still, the temperature remained in the fifties during the day, and the weak sun did little to warm us up. I guessed we would just freeze to death if we had to rely on them for winter coats. As soon as we walked outside, the wind cut through the thin material of my scrubs, making me shiver.

Everyone split into groups, shoulders hunched against the wind, but at least we were outside in the fresh air. To the right was the outside of the greenhouse where we had group, so I realized this was the ugly garden I'd seen earlier. Another group of patients was in there now. A girl named Tiffany walked over to the cracked cherub fountain and sat down beside it, wrapping her arms around herself. She stared down into the concrete basin like it wasn't completely empty of water.

A six-foot privacy fence surrounded the backyard, and the only gate had a padlock on it. Behind the fence stood a line of thick evergreen trees that blocked the view. There was no barbed wire or anything to make the fence electrified, but it still looked like it would be nearly impossible to escape—not that anyone seemed like they wanted to at the moment.

Aaron and another boy with closely cropped hair started throwing a football back and forth. I watched for a moment as the ball sailed smoothly through the air. I wondered what got Aaron sent here. Was he depressed? Anxious like me? Surely not psychotic—he didn't seem on the verge of losing it like the girl with the shaved head. His body seemed toned, even under the scrubs, so I doubted he had some sort of eating disorder.

"Hey," Katelyn called to me from the bench she, Danny, and Becca sat on. "Come over to our nail-painting station." She held a bottle of nail polish aloft. "We only have one color, and it's hideous, but it gives us something to do."

Becca waggled her bright green fingernails for me to see. "You can have green nails like us. Then you'll be an official member of our cult," she said with a wink.

Danny looked at her askance. "Cult? What in the world are you talking about now?"

She waved him off. "Inside joke."

I smiled as I walked toward them, but before I could sit on the bench, another mental health tech called my name.

"Yes?" I said, turning toward her.

Her badge said her name was Nora. With her hair cut close to her head, fuchsia glasses that sparkled, and rainbow-colored Crocs on her feet, I applauded her style choices. At least it brought some color to this place.

"You have a session with Dr. Williams scheduled now. Will you come with me?"

My shoulders dropped as the energy drained out

of me almost instantly. I didn't think I'd have to deal with him again so soon.

"We'll catch you later, Sadie," Becca called.

I nodded and followed Nora back into the building. A wave of heat hit me, and I had to take off my jacket. After being in the cold outdoors, it felt like being plunged into the depths of hell. *Appropriate,* I thought.

A flash of movement caught my attention before we made it down the bleak hallway. Someone peeked their head around the corner just ahead, and I recognized Millie by her glasses and short stature. Just as it struck me as strange—why was she hiding behind the corner?—we passed an alcove where two techs were talking. A surprised laugh bubbled up inside me. So, Millie was a spy? I supposed it must be easy for her, being so small and quiet. But before I could think further, we arrived at Dr. Williams's office.

His door stood open, and as Nora held out her hand for me to go ahead, I reluctantly walked inside.

"Sadie, I'm so glad to see you," Dr. Williams said from behind his desk. Papers and files cluttered the surface. One of the drawers of his file cabinet stood partially open, and I wished I could see the contents. I was morbidly curious about what my own file said.

Several framed documents hung above the cabinet, but a glare prevented me from seeing what they were. Probably his credentials or something.

He stood and came around to the sitting area with the beat-up leather chair and threadbare couch. "Won't you have a seat?"

I did as he asked, crossing my arms over my chest while I tried unsuccessfully to keep my leg from bouncing. He took a seat across from me in the chair.

"I understand you had a difficult first night here," Dr. Williams said, squinting at me in what he must have thought was a sympathetic way.

"I guess," I said.

"Do you want to talk about what led you to get so upset in the bathroom?"

"Not really."

Dr. Williams just watched me for a moment until I squirmed a bit in my seat. "Now remember, your treatment here is dependent on you. If you don't share how you're feeling and work with us, we can't help you, and you'll be here longer."

I lifted my head from where I'd been staring at the ugly floral pattern of the rug. "I don't know what you want me to say."

"I just want you to tell me in your own words what happened."

I heaved a sigh. "I felt trapped in a nightmare or something. Like if I couldn't see my reflection, it meant I wasn't even really there."

"I can see how that would send you into a panic," he said, jotting something down on his notepad. "I wonder, though, if you understand that the type of thinking you're describing is delusional. Just because you couldn't see yourself didn't mean you weren't there anymore."

"Of course I understand that. That's just how I felt."

"It's not a strange thing to be dealing with distorted or magical-type thinking when you have the type of diagnosis you do." He looked down at his notes on me. "You seem to have a history of a strong imagination, is that right?"

"Yes, I've always been told that." Everyone from my parents to teachers to shrinks had told me that. Most of the time, they meant it in an insulting way. Like a "you just dreamed that up because you're crazy" sort of way.

"And that's not necessarily bad. The important part is to be able to distinguish fantasy from reality. Do you feel like that's a struggle for you?"

I shrugged and focused on a loose thread on my scrub pants. I could tell reality from my imagination.

The trouble was, no one in authority ever believed me.

"Let's go back to what originally upset you. I want you to be comfortable here because that's the only way you're going to feel relaxed enough to open up and work on the things that are bothering you. My question for you is: how can we help you feel less trapped?"

I snorted. "Can you replace all the ridiculous metal mirrors with real ones? Can you tell your techs not to sedate me like an animal next time I get upset?"

"I do hate that you had to be given a chemical restraint." He shifted in his chair. "But let's talk about the mirrors. What about them triggered you?"

My jaw tightened. "They made me feel like I'm locked in an insane asylum. Like I can't even be trusted with glass."

"This is a psychiatric rehabilitation facility," Dr. Williams said. "So you can rest assured that you're not in an insane asylum."

I narrowed my eyes at him. "Calling it something different doesn't change what it is."

"And this upsets you because you feel like you shouldn't be here?"

"Wouldn't anyone who was wrongly imprisoned act a little crazy?" I countered.

He didn't look impressed. "I can understand feeling trapped when you first get here, certainly. It sounds like you quickly became overwhelmed by emotions of fear and anxiety. What about your thoughts? You already mentioned that not seeing a reflection made you feel like you weren't even there. Have you noticed an increase in irrational or magical thinking since we last spoke?"

My mind immediately summoned the images of Katelyn dead in her room that had taken hold of me during group. No way in hell was I telling Dr. Williams about that. I was pretty sure it fell into both the "irrational" and "magical thinking" categories. I could picture his reaction: his eyebrows rising as he furiously made notes on his pad—probably adding an antipsychotic to my list of meds.

"No," I said, forcing myself to meet his gaze so he wouldn't think I was lying.

He consulted his notes. "Dr. Mendez noticed that you seemed distressed during group. Did someone say something that upset you?"

"I would think anyone with a functioning conscience would feel upset listening to that shit. You might think it's easy to listen to trauma that other kids went through, but I don't."

He gave me a penetrating look through his thick-rimmed glasses, and I had to try not to avert my gaze. "Did it remind you of what happened to your sister?"

I jerked back as my heart rate ratcheted up. The terrible memory of the smell of smoke and screams filled my mind.

"I don't like thinking about that night."

"You've made that very clear," he said with a sympathetic frown. "However, the only way to deal with trauma is to talk about it. You've heard, perhaps, the saying, 'the only way to get through hell is to keep going'? That's how it is with grief and trauma. It can feel like you'll never make it to the other side—to the light at the end. But the more you talk about it and process your feelings, the better you will feel. I ask you this next question, then, knowing it will be hard to answer. If you want to get better, though, this is how we need to start. So, how did Amber die?"

The roar of flames filled my ears, and I put my hands up to cover them as if I could block out the sound. He had me in a corner—I could either talk about my psychic feelings regarding Katelyn, or I could relive my sister's death.

"How did she die?" he repeated, and I flinched.

"In a fire," I said through gritted teeth.

He nodded, like he already knew the answer. "And you survived?"

"Obviously!"

"How does that make you feel?"

This was another shrink question that made me want to scream in frustration. They always knew the answer before I responded because any idiot could figure out that surviving the fire that killed my sister made me sick with guilt.

I glared at him.

"Now, I know you think that may be an obvious answer, but there are many ways you could feel. Guilt, yes. But why? Because you survived and she didn't? Because you feel relieved you're alive? Or does it have to do with what you told me before— that you somehow blame yourself for her death?"

His words hit me harder than I would have thought possible, and I leaned back, considering. After a moment, I said, "I'm responsible for her death because I knew it was going to happen, and I didn't do anything to stop it."

"You knew there would be a fire?"

I nodded, tears stinging my eyes. "I saw my sister burning before it happened that night, and it felt so real I could smell the smoke."

Dr. Williams gently pushed the box of tissues closer to me, but I ignored it. He steepled his hands beneath his chin. "Our minds are powerful, you know. Capable of incredible feats of ingenuity, especially when we've been through trauma. Sometimes, our minds can even alter our memories and make us believe something is true when it isn't."

I curled my hands into fists. "You don't understand what I'm saying. I saw my sister die in a fire the day before a blaze swallowed our house and killed her. It was so real that it was like replaying memories of something that had already happened. I could have warned her."

"Then why didn't you?" Dr. Williams asked, clearly deciding to humor me. "Warn her, I mean. If you had this horrible premonition that she would burn to death in a fire, why didn't you say something?"

"Because of what you said before—my imagination. All my life, my family has rolled their eyes and told me I was being dramatic. That all the things I told them about were just dreamed up in my head; it was 'just my imagination.' It didn't take long for me to realize that was code for 'she's crazy.'"

I took a shuddered breath. "I couldn't stand to hear them call me that again, so I just . . . kept it to myself. I knew my sister would die, and I didn't even talk to her that night."

I only remembered bits and pieces of the day before the fire. Amber brushing past me in the hallway without saying a word because she was on the phone. Her door closed behind her with a click, and I heard the lock engage so I wouldn't try to come in. My room was right next to hers, and she kept laughing so loudly I turned my music up to drown her out, but I could still hear her. Eventually, I went and told Mom to shut her up. I had a huge exam in the morning, and I hadn't studied.

I never ended up taking it, anyway.

Some of the residual anger from that night snuck into my thoughts, and I flushed with shame. Amber was always leaving me out. Always pushing me away. She and her friends made fun of me behind my back, and a lot of times, to my face. Had I intentionally kept that premonition from her? Had some small, horrible part of me not cared?

These were the thoughts that tortured me. I

couldn't speak them out loud to Dr. Williams, though. I didn't want anyone to know.

When I cried about Amber now, it was for the Amber she was before becoming a teenager. The one who would stay up late with me talking and giggling like we were best friends at a sleepover instead of sisters. The girl who used to paint and do art with me, before mean friends and boys and everything else got in the way.

Before she started hating me.

You're such a psycho, she'd say, her lip curled and her eyes flashing. *We're all embarrassed by you.*

"Sadie?" Dr. Williams's voice interrupted the ghost of my sister in my head. "Are you remembering something?"

"No." I was done with this conversation. I wanted to go home, but of course, that wasn't an option anymore. I would settle for just getting the hell out of this room.

"We're going to work through this, okay?" When I didn't say anything, he leaned toward me. "You're going to get better."

"Sure, all right," I muttered. "Can I go now?"

"Yes. But remember, the more you put in the effort to talk about things that are bothering you, the faster you'll improve."

I paused on my way out the door. "And then I can leave this place? Like Lisa?"

My toxic trait was that I liked to mess with people. See their reaction. Stir the pot. And ever since my new friends had hinted that something strange had happened to Lisa, I was curious about how Dr. Williams would react.

He stilled, and ever so slowly put down his pen. "Lisa?"

"Yeah, the girl that used to be in my room?"

He blinked owlishly at me. "Who told you about her?"

"Katelyn mentioned her today," I said, feigning nonchalance. So even Dr. Williams tensed up when I mentioned this girl. Was she like the one in the dining room, losing her mind as she screamed and threw stuff? And how much would that suck to be the black sheep of this place? The one no one wants to talk about?

"I see," Dr. Williams said, lips pinched like he was constipated.

"Will I be able to leave like she did?"

He seemed to shake off whatever weirdo psychiatrist stupor he was in. "If you put in the work, yes. You won't be here forever, Sadie. That, I can promise you."

I didn't want to hash anything else out with him, so I just nodded and walked away.

Talking through the premonition about Amber only made me think of my most recent feeling about Katelyn. What if it came true again?

If I couldn't even warn my own sister, then how was I supposed to warn someone I just met?

And what would happen if I didn't?

7

Sometimes at home, the thoughts in my head just got too intense, and all I could handle doing was watching TV. The more mindless, the better. I couldn't draw or paint or do anything creative. I just had to sit and stare at a screen for a while, and then I could function again. I had a small TV that sat on a desk in my room. One I had bought with my own money. Sometimes I would watch it at night to help me fall asleep. I just turned on some lame reality show on Netflix and let it run until the screen came up asking if I was still watching it. By then, I had usually been asleep for an hour.

After that session with Dr. Williams, all I wanted was to check out in front of a screen. My mind felt fuzzy, like it had been working too hard. *Emotional fatigue.* That phrase floated through my head, a left-over from some past therapy session. You could experience emotions so strongly that they tired you out. I had felt it before, just being around my family.

I started toward my room before realizing I had nothing there. No TV. No laptop. No phone.

Dragging my feet with a groan, I turned back toward the communal room. There was a TV in there, I knew, but it was a small one that everyone had to cluster around. Laughter and raised voices spilled out of the room the closer I got, and my shoulders dropped. Having a bunch of other kids around talking nonstop was the opposite of what I was going for.

One look at the TV, and my hopes further collapsed. It clearly only had a cheap cable package —no streaming, no HBO or even YouTube, like I was used to. Some sort of boring crime-solving drama was on, and by the way everyone was debating who the killer was, I knew they'd never let me change it.

With a sigh, I dropped into the chair farthest away—one of those uncomfortable hospital waiting room models that were designed to last a hundred years by people who gave two shits about your comfort. None of the kids I talked to before were in here. I recognized a few from group, but I didn't know any of them well enough to try to strike up a conversation. Not that I was in the mood for that, anyway.

When I looked around the room again, I noticed Millie sitting curled up in a chair, reading a book. I just hadn't seen her the first time around. I wondered how many times she was overlooked like that, being so small and quiet. She looked peaceful—not happy, but at least calm and content for the moment. It was probably impossible to be happy in this place.

I turned back to the TV. The cops on the show were overacting, and I had arrived too late to follow which clues they were investigating, so my mind started to wander.

I thought about my own little mystery that was starting to form here—about this Lisa person. Katelyn said she hadn't left. Or she'd said, "not exactly." Whatever that meant. Dr. Williams had never admitted she left either. Was it like some kind of *Jane Eyre* situation where the girl was locked up in the attic? A chill crept down my spine at the thought. This place certainly had a gothic vibe, and there was something off about Dr. Williams. Maybe he secretly locked up kids he couldn't "fix" just like Mr. Rochester kept his mentally ill wife in the attic.

The others had warned me off Aaron, but I bet he knew more about Lisa. He'd dated her, supposedly. What had Becca said? That I was the type of girl Aaron attached himself to? I tossed that thought around in my head for a minute, but it wasn't helpful. How could someone know what type of person they were to someone else? I knew for a fact that the way I saw myself was definitely not how others saw me.

Tell me about yourself, my old shrink had said to me a million years ago.

I'm into art and drawing, I had said, almost cheerfully back then. *I'm pretty extroverted and make friends easily.*

My shrink had snorted out a laugh. *You? Extroverted? You know that's when you like being around other people, right?*

The smile had fallen from my face. *Yes, I know what it means. I like hanging out with my friends.*

He'd just continued smirking at me, until my mood had turned dark and ugly, like a sudden summer thunderstorm.

The truth is, he said, holding my gaze like he was about to impart something really profound, *you don't have any friends. That's one of the reasons you're here.*

Obviously, I hadn't worked with that psychiatrist

long. He had this impression of me, and he refused to hear anything else. But doctors were like that. Super arrogant with a savior complex. They believed they were smarter than everyone else, and it didn't help that most adults saw them that way, too. It took months of begging before my parents let me switch therapists because they believed him over me.

So who knew what these other kids saw when they looked at me. They were bound to be more perceptive than some egotistical psychiatrist, though. I thought of my short conversations with Aaron. His voice was warm and comforting, and he hadn't creeped me out or made me feel like maybe I should lock my bedroom door at night (you know, if we were even allowed to have locks). I've always trusted my instincts about people.

That's why when an icy cold sensation washed over me about Katelyn during group, like I was coming down with the flu, I didn't ignore it. What I didn't understand was how something bad could happen to her here. They took everything away from us that we could possibly harm ourselves with, and she didn't seem suicidal to me. I thought of the girl in the dining room who had to be sedated. How often did other kids hurt each other here? Surely if a kid had a violent background, they wouldn't just let them wander around with the rest of us.

That same sick feeling progressed until I had chills. My teeth chattered and I rubbed my arms. All around me, kids were still talking or watching TV. I didn't like feeling sick and vulnerable in front of other people, so I started to head back to my room. Even if Millie decided to go back there, too, I didn't have to worry about her talking and asking a bunch of questions.

I hurried down the hall with my head down to avoid making eye contact with anyone.

Before I could pass Dr. Williams's office, the door opened, and Katelyn practically burst out of it. I only caught a glimpse of her face before she hurried away, but tears streamed down in dark streaks from her eye makeup running.

My stomach plummeted at the sight of her. Did Dr. Williams call her in there after what I told him about Lisa?

It made me ashamed to admit this, but a huge part of me just wanted to continue to my room and hide. For about thirty seconds, I hovered in the hallway. Should I just let it go? It might have nothing to do with me. But the timing seemed pretty suspicious, and if Dr. Williams had yelled at her and made her cry because of me, then I couldn't just ignore it. If I was the one who got her in trouble, I at least owed her an apology.

I didn't know exactly where her room was, but all the girls were on the same floor, so I just went down the hall until I found a door with her name on it. It wasn't far from my room, and it made me pause for a moment. Didn't she say she hadn't heard a scream that night? She told me her room was a few doors down, but she was much closer than I had pictured. If I had heard something, she should have, too.

Okay, I fully admit this next thought was totally paranoid, but it grabbed hold of my mind anyway. What if she *had* heard the scream and just wanted to make me look crazy? It wouldn't be the first time this had happened to me. My own sister used to make it her goal in life to gaslight me until I cried. Just little things that would get under my skin. Like she'd sneak into my room and hide my stuff, or take my clothes and then say they had always been hers and ask what the hell I was smoking.

Katelyn isn't Amber, I told myself.

I took a deep breath and knocked on her door. No movement came from inside, so I tried again. "Katelyn? It's Sadie."

I waited, but she never came to the door.

It only made my gnawing anxiety chew my insides harder. I wanted to apologize and resolve it. Otherwise, I would dread seeing her the next day.

I stood outside her door much longer than was probably normal before finally giving up and turning back toward my own room.

My jaw started to hurt, and I realized it was because I had it clenched so tight. I hated that I didn't get to talk to her. I thought again about how oddly Dr. Williams had reacted to my mention of Lisa. If he really had yelled at Katelyn just because I told him what she'd said at lunch, it seemed like an extreme reaction. Why couldn't anyone talk about Lisa? Where was Lisa?

Millie wasn't in our room, so I flopped down on my bed facedown with a groan. As the thoughts buzzed around in my head nonstop, I knew I was in for a rough night.

I just really wished Katelyn had opened the door.

You know that feeling where reality is fuzzy around the edges, so you know it's a dream? Ever since I was little, I had enough self-awareness in my dreams that I could control things that happened in them. Even wake myself up if it was a nightmare. But I sometimes had these dreams that grabbed hold of me so hard I couldn't break away.

The last time I'd had a dream like that was the night before my sister died.

And I was in the midst of another one right now.

In my dream, I stood outside Katelyn's door. I could tell it was the middle of the night because the lights in the hallway were off. Only the nightlights provided illumination at regular intervals. It upped the creep factor significantly, raising the hairs on the back of my neck. I tried to concentrate hard in my dream to turn on the lights, but nothing happened.

The next thing I knew, I was inside her room. Without even understanding why, my heart pounded away. Katelyn was curled up in her bed to my left, snoring gently. I turned to look at her roommate's side of the room, but she wasn't there. The rest of the room was empty and quiet. I thought about everything I wanted to say to her earlier, about Dr. Williams calling her into his office and about Lisa, but no words came out of my mouth.

Instead, I took a few steps closer to her bed until I was looming over her. In my dream, I reached down, but when I looked at my hands, they didn't look like my own. They were bigger and stronger. But it was like I couldn't see them clearly. I couldn't tell if they had a lot of hair like a man's hands, or maybe even painted nails like a woman might have. I just knew in that way of dreams that they weren't mine.

The whole atmosphere of the dream changed then, from mildly creepy and anxiety-provoking to full-on dark and nightmarish. A scream built inside me that couldn't be released.

Those hands wrapped around Katelyn's throat, and her eyes flew open. Under her eyes was smudged from mascara, and the whites were bloodshot from crying. I was so close I could see the ring of brown around the pupils in her hazel eyes.

Katelyn would have screamed, but the hands around her throat made that impossible.

I tried to scream again—for help, for the nightmare to end, for anything but to witness this. It was like I was trapped behind glass. All I could do was watch.

Her face turned red as she fought and bucked on the bed. But the hands were stronger. They held her down. They cut off her air.

No, I thought, *this can't be happening.*

Katelyn's color changed from red to purple, and then her writhing grew slower.

Katelyn, no!

But then her movements stopped altogether. Her hands fell to her sides, still curled in claws to try fending off her attacker.

A blood vessel in her eye had popped, turning the white to red.

Her eyes stayed open, unseeing.

8

I awoke with a coughing fit, a stifled scream stuck in my throat like a bone. It took a moment to realize I was still in my room. When I looked for Millie, her side was empty. She had made the bed before leaving the room, the blankets straightened with the stuffed dog lying against her pillow.

A dream, I told myself. *Just a dream.*

Or was it a premonition? Did it mean that something would happen to Katelyn? What if she was being murdered right now? I rubbed my arms as I sat up to ward off a sudden chill.

In my mind, I shoved that line of thinking into a locked box and put it away. It was just a dream. People had them all the time. Sometimes they were weird or disturbing, but that didn't mean anything. Like that one messed-up dream I had one time where I kissed my math teacher. It didn't mean I actually wanted to, especially since he was pasty white and looked like a frog.

I got up, grabbed another pair of ugly scrubs to change into after a shower, and went to the bathroom. Two of the shower stalls were occupied. After gathering some basic supplies from the cabinet, I showered quickly.

While I brushed my teeth, I avoided looking at the fake mirrors and almost tricked myself into thinking I was at a normal place—maybe a summer camp or something. A summer camp where instead of getting to do fun activities inside, I had to line up for meds like a prisoner and go to endless talk therapy sessions. Super fun.

I dutifully made my way to the nurse's station for my meds because I wanted Dr. Williams to see that I was making an effort. It took me a few moments to realize how everyone around me was acting because I had been stuck in my own head and trying to be the model mental patient.

My first clue was that there wasn't a line for meds. Everyone clustered around each other, looking pale and shaken. The sound of uncontrollable sobbing drew my attention to a corner of the room where a few kids were unsuccessfully trying to comfort Danny. He cried with painful abandon, barely able to hold himself upright.

A grim-faced Dr. Williams appeared from the hallway that led to his office. He seemed to assess the situation quickly before saying, "Help Danny to his room," to one of the nearby mental health techs. She put her arm around his shoulders and gently steered him toward the stairs.

I watched it all with a sinking feeling in my stomach.

Then I felt a hand on my shoulder. I turned to find Becca with red-rimmed eyes. "They found Katelyn dead in her room."

Even though I had been afraid of this ever since my dream, hearing it still knocked me back a step. Tears rushed to my eyes as I replayed the horrible nightmare in my mind.

Katelyn's eyes widened as strong hands wrap around her throat.

Her face turned that horrible shade of mottled purple.

Her eyes bulged until finally they stayed open and unseeing.

So that disturbing nightmare had happened in *real life*? How could this happen again?

That terrible sensation I had yesterday, followed by the bad dream, meant that I really could predict someone's death. I never wanted to be more wrong in my life.

A wave of nausea hit me so strongly I broke out in a sweat. I had to swallow hard to keep from throwing up and was thankful I hadn't had breakfast yet.

If Katelyn died, then had I witnessed her murder in my dream?

I thought of the way Katelyn left Dr. Williams's office in tears. What did that mean?

More importantly, who killed her?

***

Julia had appeared and gathered all the kids into the group therapy room. Counting the patients in other groups, twenty-four of us called this psych facility home. Normally, they split us up, but when all of us gathered together, we took up the whole room. No sharing circle like last time. We were shoulder to shoulder in here. The only person missing was Danny. I didn't know him that well yet, but I had a feeling he and Katelyn were close.

I sat next to Becca, and my muscles quivered like I'd just downed two Red Bulls in succession. I kept awkwardly bumping into her. She didn't seem to notice, though.

I leaned forward, and Aaron caught my eye. He was sitting just a couple of kids down from me, and his expression mirrored everyone else's. We were all in shock. Katelyn had just been laughing and eating with the rest of us yesterday. How could she be dead?

Julia stood at the front of the room and cleared her throat gently. Today she had on a beaded necklace in the bright shade of coral. I couldn't take my eyes off it. I would rather look at that than the sympathy etched on her face.

"My friends," she said in a gentle voice that somehow still carried across the room. The few whispers and murmurs stopped until we all fell silent. "You already heard the terrible news that Katelyn passed away last night, and I know you all have questions. We're still investigating to find out exactly what happened and why, but what we know so far is that Katelyn committed suicide."

The air was sucked from the room as everyone stared at each other in a shocked stupor.

"We understand that hearing about such a

terrible outcome for someone whom you've gotten to know closely can be devastating. All of us therapists will be available at any time for the next week for you to talk, even if it's the middle of the night. We don't want anyone to deal with grief on their own."

"They don't want someone else killing themselves," Becca muttered beside me.

Julia launched into a monologue about grief, but my own thoughts tripped over each other to the point that I couldn't concentrate. Suicide. It didn't match up with my dream, and I wondered if they were lying. Or did I have it all wrong? Maybe the main point of my dream was that she would die, not that she'd die by someone strangling her.

Suddenly, the most inappropriate desire to shout out a question overtook me. I had to resist the urge to ask for details of her death. Super nosy questions had a time and a place, and I knew everyone would look at me strangely if I asked in the middle of group.

"I'll stay in this room for the next hour in case any of you would like to talk now," Julia said, wrapping up this sad meeting.

Maybe she would give me some answers so I wouldn't have to shout in front of everyone like I had Tourette syndrome.

Before anyone else could move toward Julia, I went to her side as many of the others filed out of the room.

Julia's eyes were round with sympathy as she looked at me. "Did you want to stay and talk about it, Sadie?"

I nodded.

"Okay," she told me before turning back to the stragglers still in the room. "I'm going to talk with Sadie first, and if anyone else wants to speak to me, you can wait in a line outside the room. I'll spend time with anyone who needs me."

When the room had cleared, Julia gestured for me to take a seat across from her.

"I'm so sorry, Sadie," Julia said, her hands clasped in her lap. "I know you and Katelyn seemed to get along well."

"I just can't believe it," I said.

Julia sighed and nodded. "Truthfully, it came as a shock to all of us. She only had a few days left here."

My head jerked up at that. "Then why——"

"I wish I had a better answer for you. It could have been that the thought of leaving triggered her instead of making her feel hopeful and excited. I know she experienced some feelings of being overwhelmed and nervous, but that happens a lot when kids get ready to leave here. For whatever reason, she must not have felt comfortable enough to tell one of us that she had suicidal thoughts. That part is what really worries me."

"I don't understand how it even happened," I said. "We don't even have anything to hurt ourselves with in this place."

"It hasn't happened many times over the years, but it does happen, unfortunately."

"How did she do it?" I asked, twisting the bottom of my shirt in my hands.

"Oh, honey," she said with a shake of her head. "You don't want to know all the gruesome details."

How psychotic would I sound if I said I did? "It can't be any worse than what I'm imagining," I said truthfully.

"It's not my place to tell you," she said, and I gritted my teeth.

It was clear she planned to continue stonewalling me, so I just needed to end the conversation.

"I don't think this has really sunk in yet," I said. And I didn't have to fake the way my voice wavered.

Julia reached out and touched my hand. "I'm sure you're still in shock."

I nodded tearfully. "I think I need to go back to my room now, if that's okay."

"Of course. I'll be here if you want to talk again."

I thanked her and left, but instead of heading back toward my room, I went in search of Becca. Maybe she'd know something. She wouldn't refuse to tell me like Julia had.

When I got to the rec room, kids were in subdued clusters, whispering about what had happened. After scanning faces, I found Becca talking to Millie and Aaron.

"This is just so fucked up," Becca was saying, her eyes flashing. "It makes no sense at all why'd she do this."

"You didn't see it coming either?" I asked.

"No, not when the girl had like, three days left here. Even if she was suicidal again, and she sure as hell didn't seem like it to me, why would she do it here?"

Millie nodded, and Aaron spoke up. "Exactly. It's much harder here with nothing but like, bedsheets."

I shot him a confused look. "Wait, bedsheets? What do you mean?"

"She hung herself," Becca said with a terse shake of her head. "I overheard the nurses talking about it. She tied her sheet around the light fixture in her room."

I stood there with one hand on the way to my mouth, but my mind raced along so fast I couldn't even finish the gesture.

She hung herself.

She wasn't strangled in her bed.

The dream may not have gotten the circumstances right, but it was still hard to ignore that I had a dream she died, and the next day, she was dead. Did it matter how?

"I'm not surprised something like that happened," Aaron said, his expression shadowed. "This place gets to you."

"I guess," Becca said with a skeptical sneer. "But again, she was going to *leave* in three days!"

They continued to low-key argue about Katelyn's death when a horrible thought popped into my mind:

What if Katelyn really had been strangled, but the killer made it look like suicide?

9

By the time art therapy rolled around in the late afternoon, my own thoughts sickened me so much that I was ready to throw myself into painting. Maybe then I could stop the constant stream of consciousness that was my brain.

Art took place in a converted sunroom at the back of the big house. Just walking into the room made my chest feel lighter. The smell of paint and all the colorful patient artwork on display tricked my mind into thinking I was just at a normal art school. All the windows let in a ton of natural light, which eliminated the need for harsh, overhead lighting. Whoever first built this mansion must have really liked brightly lit rooms. I didn't know of another house that had both an attached greenhouse and a sunroom.

Dried paint in no discernible pattern covered the cheap, foldable tables in the room. It reminded me of the art lessons I used to take—before my sister died. They took place at my town's cultural center because my parents were too cheap to get me private lessons. They spent most of their money on Amber. The art teacher there had been pretty good, though. She taught me about shading and mediums, lighting and perspective, and all the different types of art supplies. I had a talent for it, but I hadn't been able to draw or paint since the fire.

Becca wasn't in this class at the same time as me, but Aaron and his roommate Jon were. I took an easel next to them and tried to listen to the art therapist while my hands itched to put paint to paper.

"Hey there, y'all, I'm Shandra," the therapist said, twisting her thick, curly hair into a bun on top of her head. Frizzy pieces had escaped around her face and nape of her neck, flecked with paint. "We had some upsetting news this morning."

Everyone made sad murmured sounds of agreement.

"As soon as I heard that, I set up the easels. There's no better way to express your thoughts and grief than through a blank canvas. Try not to think about what you want to paint, but instead, let your brush pull those feelings from you. Better out than in, yeah? If you're feeling sad, frustrated, anxious, or even angry, this is the perfect way to vent safely."

I'd only been half-listening until her gaze zeroed in on mine, and I could see the hint of green in her brown eyes. "Because remember: our emotions are natural, but the way we express them needs to be healthy and constructive. Paint on paper instead of punching walls, right?"

Aaron and Jon nodded beside me. I guess they could relate to that, though I'd never had the desire to break my hand by putting it through Sheetrock.

Finally, she let us get started. I glanced down at the paint on the shelf of my easel. Bottles of cheap acrylics, an assortment of brushes, and a plastic palette filled the space. I definitely wouldn't be creating a masterpiece with these supplies, but they could at least serve the purpose of helping me de-stress. I loaded up my palette with the darkest colors: black, blue, green. By mixing with black, I made the blue and green darker still. Bright white became ashy gray, until my entire palette was filled with the colors of night and shadows.

I tried to follow Shandra's advice and just let my

brush flow. I started by painting the entire canvas with the ashy gray before layering on deeper shadows. I left a circle of light near the top of the canvas bright white with the deepest black just underneath it. At the bottom, I worked on a crouched figure gazing up at the light.

Images from my nightmare kept popping into my head, and I grimaced. How could I tell anyone about it? Last time I'd done that, I got a one-way ticket to this place. I could practically hear Dr. Williams's reaction now: *you suffer from an overactive imagination, Sadie.* I mean, maybe that was true, but there was no doubt I had the dream. I could remember standing in front of her bedroom door and watching her sleep like it was a movie. How would he explain that? That I dreamed her death before it happened?

He just wouldn't believe me. That's how he would explain it away. He would treat me like everyone always did: like I was insane.

When I stepped back to look at my painting, my gaze shifted to what the other kids in the room were working on. Everyone else had used bright colors and painted abstracts or nature scenes. Their canvases were filled with reds and oranges and yellows. Beside me, Jon had attempted to paint a kid playing soccer, but the figure was crude and childish.

"Whoa, Sadie," Jon said, his gaze drawn to my painting. "That is some dark shit you painted. What even is that?"

Heat creeped up my neck when I saw that Aaron was looking at it, too. "It's a girl trapped in a well." I had made the whole canvas look like the stone sides of the dark well, with moonlight coming from far above the girl at the bottom. She gazed up at it from below, knowing she had no chance of escape.

"It's amazing," Aaron said, coming to my side.

"Amazingly disturbing," Jon said, but in that elbow-to-the-side way that was supposed to be joking.

Aaron's face darkened like a cloud blotting out the sun. "Dude, shut up."

I tried not to let myself be annoyed. Jon didn't seem to be trying to insult me. "Well, I'm not feeling super happy today after finding out about Katelyn."

"Seriously," Aaron said with a sympathetic nod and a quelling look at Jon, who turned back to clean up his paint. "That was pretty messed up."

"It was a nightmare," I said, making an unintentional pun that he wouldn't pick up on. "But what did you mean when you said this place gets to you?"

A muscle in his jaw flexed like I had asked an uncomfortable question. "It can just feel more like a prison than a rehab center, you know? And when you're trapped, you can act desperate."

I glanced at my painting of the girl trapped in the well. He had pinpointed exactly how I felt. I couldn't tell anyone about my dream without sounding crazy, so I was stuck.

"Does this place feel like a prison to you?"

His eyes met mine, and I felt a jolt like a little static shock. "It didn't used to." His gaze dropped to my mouth as he took a tiny step forward.

I found myself leaning toward him as if by some unseen magnetism. But a flash of hurt crossed his face—like I had rejected him—and he pulled back. With a small shake of his head, he turned and walked away.

I went over and over what I had said and how we'd been standing in relation to each other, but I had no explanation for his sudden departure. My cheeks heated with a blush as I surreptitiously glanced around to see if anyone had noticed. Everyone was busy cleaning up their paints and palettes, so I did the same.

It wasn't until I'd put my paints up that I finally noticed Aaron's painting, still sitting on the easel beside Jon's.

It was of a girl hanging from a light fixture in her room.

T hat night, I thought I would be too afraid to go to sleep. Too afraid of prophetic dreams or even just a run-of-the-mill nightmare of Katelyn killing herself. But all those thoughts and emotions made me feel like I'd just finished a marathon, and I collapsed into my bed, completely exhausted. I had maybe two thoughts before succumbing to oblivion.

Sadie.

"Sadie!"

I awoke with a gasp and a jerk in the middle of the night to Becca's hand on my shoulder. I could barely make out her face and messy hair in the dim light of my room. I sat up quickly.

"Please tell me no one else died," I said in a rush, looking around for Millie and letting out a breath when I saw her already up and dressed.

"No, but we're having a memorial for Katelyn. You coming?"

"Now?"

Becca groaned. "Yes, *now*. You think I'm waking

you up at three a.m. for fun? This is when night shift usually falls asleep on the job."

Millie nodded and waved at me to get up and get dressed. I put on the same tired scrubs I'd worn earlier and followed them both down to the kitchen.

The house became even creepier at night. Dim lighting cast everything in deep shadow. Instead of the constant background noise of kids talking, nurses and techs running around, and the TV blaring, there was only the occasional hum from the AC unit.

As we snuck past the nurse's station, I saw that Becca had been totally right about night shift. One of the male nurses slept so hard I could hear his snores from here. We didn't even have to keep our footfalls that quiet as we passed by.

I winced once we entered the bright kitchen after being in the dark of the rest of the house. Every one of the ugly overhead fluorescent lights blazed, reflecting off the stainless-steel work surface of the industrial countertops. This was nothing like our kitchen at home, with its butcher block island, cluttered counters, and cheesy farm animal artwork all over the walls, even though we didn't even own a dog —much less farm animals. The space here was sterile and clearly made for churning out a lot of disgusting hospital-style food. I could still smell the lingering scent of onions.

Everything was super-sized, too, like this was a kitchen for giants. Two huge refrigerators dominated the space, and even the double kitchen sink looked like it could be used to bathe children instead of dishes. Four ovens took up one whole wall, and two dishwashers hummed loudly. An entire wall of cabinets spanned from the ceiling to the floor. Some of them had glass fronts, and I could see rows of dusty-looking drinking glasses inside. They looked old enough to have been original to the house.

Five kids milled around the kitchen, but I only knew three of them. Aaron and Jon were talking with Danny, while two girls chatted with clear plastic cups of what looked like lemonade in their hands. When they saw the three of us walk in, they called out quiet greetings.

Seeing Aaron for the first time since art therapy made my heart race, but I didn't know why. I couldn't deny being attracted to him, and I certainly didn't mind his attention. But I would be lying to myself if I didn't admit that his artwork had freaked me out. Why paint something like that? Seeing him here with everyone else for Katelyn's memorial made me doubt my initial reaction to it, though. Art therapy was supposed to be a way to deal with your thoughts and feelings in a safe way, and Katelyn's hanging weighed on all our minds.

"So glad you could drag your asses out of bed and join us," Danny said, shoving cups of lemonade toward us and interrupting my thoughts. "It's just Crystal Light," he added, waving a hand toward a large container of powdered lemonade. "It's the best we could do."

"Katelyn loved this stuff," Becca said, making a face at her cup.

"She had low lemonade standards," Danny said. He glanced at me as I took a sip of the lukewarm drink. "Sadie, I think you know most everyone here, except maybe Erin and Tamesha."

Erin was short and unassuming, while Tamesha had long braids and a wide smile. "I was Katelyn's roommate," Tamesha said.

"That must be hard," I said sympathetically. "Were you there that night?"

She shook her head. "I felt really sick after dinner, like maybe I had food poisoning. I was bouncing back and forth from the nurse's office to the bathroom." She glanced down at her cup. "I'm the one who found her in the morning, though."

I shivered when I realized it was just like my

dream. I remembered Tamesha's side of the room being empty.

"I'm so sorry," I said, a sudden lump in my throat making it hard to swallow. "That had to have been traumatic."

"It was messed up. The day before, we had been talking about what she was going to do when she got out." Tamesha scratched her arm, and I saw she had red marks there. "I guess she was faking all that or something."

"Okay," Danny said with a clap to draw our attention, "no more of that. We're here to talk about all our good memories of Katelyn—not make ourselves depressed over what happened yesterday." He cleared his throat and started blinking furiously. "We're just going to talk about how great she was, okay?" The sudden thick quality of his voice brought tears to my eyes. "Those are the rules."

Jon stepped forward and put his arm around Danny.

Becca put her empty cup down on the counter and gestured for Aaron to pour her some more. "I'll start then. Katelyn was the first girl who was nice to me here, but more importantly, she was the first girl who was nice to me in forever. I came from a high school full of mean, small-town bitches, so I arrived here all jaded and suspicious.

"But Katelyn didn't know about all that. She just smiled at me all big and said, 'Welcome to hell,' so cheerfully that I burst out laughing. She was silly and real and literally the nicest girl I've ever met, and I am so mad she's gone . . . I can't even . . . *so* mad that she would do this—" Danny cleared his throat in warning, so Becca reeled herself in with a deep breath.

"I get it, Kate, I do. Life's hard, and no one knows what's really going on in your head but you. Still, she was the kindest person I knew." She held up her plastic cup to toast, and we all did the same. "To Katelyn, the nicest girl gone too soon."

We repeated the toast and took sips of our lemonade.

I knew eulogies and memorials always focused on the good stuff in a person's life, but my twisted brain made me remember the rude thing Katelyn said to me the first morning I met her—about looking rough. I inwardly chastised myself for being negative. As mean comments went, that one rated lower than all the others I'd been dealt. But focusing on the negative was another one of my toxic traits. Someone could be a literal saint, and I would remember the one time they had a bad day and said something semi-mean.

"I'm going to go next while I can still talk," Danny said, smiling through his tears. He fanned his face for a second before shaking it off. "Katelyn was like a sister to me. I know this will be a total shocker to all of you, but when I first came here, I was a mess. Katelyn let me cry and bitch to my heart's content, and I swear it made me better so much faster than group therapy. She could be a mess, too, don't get me wrong. But she was also a great listener. She made me feel like she cared, you know? And I'm just really going to miss her," he said, his voice breaking again.

Jon rubbed his shoulder while Danny struggled to get his emotions under control. He held up his cup. "To Katelyn," he managed to croak out.

The others gave short little memories of Katelyn, too, but Becca and Danny clearly knew her best. Eventually, my turn came, and all I could think about was the cold premonition and horrible nightmare.

"I didn't know Katelyn long," I began haltingly, "but even in the short time I knew her, she tried to help me. Like when I asked about"—I caught myself before saying Aaron's name and flushed when I saw he was watching me—"about what to expect here. She, Becca, and Millie were right there when I was freaking out during group, saying comforting things. She didn't have to do that, but I could tell that was the kind of person she was."

Talking about that day at group reminded me suddenly of what Katelyn had said, and my monologue ground to a halt while my whole mind seized at the memory. She had talked about being scared to go home, of even going back to cutting herself. Was she so upset that she killed herself? Is that what I had picked up on in group? Maybe Katelyn had told us all that as a cry for help.

And we totally ignored her.

Everyone was staring at me, waiting for me to continue, so I held up my half-empty cup. "To Katelyn, for caring about the new girl."

"Now that toasts are done, it's time for ice cream," Becca said, rubbing her hands together.

"You're going to break into their ice cream supply?" Aaron asked with an incredulous tone.

"Yeah, why not? They never bother to feed it to us, so what's the point in all these giant tubs going to waste?"

"It's what Katelyn would have wanted," Danny said, getting out disposable bowls and spoons.

We had our choice of chocolate or vanilla, and most of us picked chocolate. It was probably the cheapest ice cream, but at the same time, it tasted like the best I ever had. My sister used to love to go to Cold Stone and pick a million mix-ins, but then she'd laugh and call me boring for just wanting plain old vanilla.

I scrunched my nose up and looked down at my bowl of chocolate. No, that wasn't right. I never ate vanilla. I must have been misremembering.

"You okay?" a warm voice said from beside me, and I looked up to see Aaron had left his small group to talk to me.

"I'm still in shock, I think. How about you? I think you probably knew her better than I did."

"I guess I just thought we were safe from that here," he said with a pained expression. "But if all these therapists aren't paying attention, then what hope do we all have of getting better?"

"That's a scary thought. I was just thinking about what Katelyn told us in group—about being scared to go home and start cutting again and all that. Julia seems nice, but maybe she should have asked her more about that?"

He nodded. "Exactly. That's why we all have to look out for each other."

"Becca said something like that to me the other day."

"I'll look out for you if you'll look out for me," he said, with a smile just touching his lips.

"Agreed," I said, and we touched our lemonade cups together.

When the memorial ended, and we all headed back to our rooms, I thought about Lisa for the first time since Katelyn died. Had they all had a sad little party for her, too? I wondered again what had happened to her and why they all acted so secretive about it. This line of thinking got me nowhere, though. No one would tell me anything about it if I asked.

The thought of Lisa reminded me that Katelyn had been the last one to try and tell me about her.

And now she was dead.

10

———

Several days after Katelyn's memorial in the kitchen, it was like her death had never happened. That seemed so callous to say. A girl had *died* and all of us just continued to go about our lives. I blamed this place, though. The daily routine lulled you into this falsely calm state—or maybe the drugs did. Either way, no more wailing and gnashing of teeth happened over her loss, and though I knew many of her friends like Danny still missed her, they had probably already gotten used to the idea that she was leaving, anyway.

The whole thing made me sick to think about, so at the urging of Dr. Williams, I forced it from my mind. I never told him about my psychic feeling and dream that she was going to die. I just didn't see the point. He would only try to convince me that my mind had made it all up. He would probably increase the antipsychotics he just put me on, and those were the meds that made me feel the worst. Tired of feeling groggy all the time, I learned to tuck the pill under my tongue and make a big show of swallowing for the nurse. She never looked closely enough to realize I didn't take it. Later, I would spit it out and toss it in a wadded-up napkin in the trash. I still took the antianxiety and antidepressant, though. They at least helped take the edge off my constant nervousness.

For my own sanity, I had to keep myself from all my what-if thoughts regarding Katelyn and Lisa. So I did what I always did: I locked them up in my mind. It helped that I had made that painting of the girl in the well during art therapy. I would picture the painting in my mind, and then I would pour all my obsessive thoughts down into the well and imagine a concrete lid dragged on top, sealing them in.

While I got my breakfast, Becca and Millie talked at a table together. Well, Becca talked. Millie smiled and nodded a lot. They had already gotten their food and eaten most of it by the time I got in line. It had been hard for me to wake up lately because as much as I tried to keep my thoughts under lock and key during the day, I couldn't control my dreams. I'd had nightmares every night since right before Katelyn died.

Jon and Danny joined the breakfast line behind me, and I smiled weakly at them.

"Hey there, darkness, my old friend," Jon said with a grin that was just this side of mean. He'd called me similar things ever since he saw my painting. I tried to think of a smart retort, but as I turned and met Jon's gaze, my whole body froze. Old people had this saying, about feeling like someone was walking over their grave. Like suddenly being drenched with a cold dread.

That was exactly what I experienced as I looked into Jon's dark blue eyes.

Not again, I thought.

"Sorry," Danny said with a shake of his head, nudging Jon in the ribs. "He can be an ass."

"I thought it would be funny," Jon said with a perturbed look. I could barely track their conversation with my heart threatening to beat out of my chest. I looked down, and my arms were covered in goosebumps.

"I've told you before that I'm like the only one who gets your humor," Danny said, leading him away while I struggled to hold on to my tray.

I didn't say anything as the cafeteria worker placed a plate full of eggs, toast, and bacon on my tray. Stiltedly, I walked over to the table with Becca and Millie. When Becca greeted me, I mumbled a hello with a smile that probably looked more like a grimace. There was only one other chair at this table, so hopefully Danny and Jon would sit somewhere else. I didn't think I could stand to look at Jon.

"You know, you can ask them to fix your meds," Becca said when I picked at my eggs. "Some of them make me eat like a horse, but sometimes they completely wipe my appetite."

"I'm just getting tired of rubber eggs," I said and summoned a fake smile.

"No one can blame you for that," Becca said with a smirk. "Millie's the only one who likes them."

Millie took a big bite for show, and Becca laughed.

Danny and Jon came over to our table, and I held my breath. "I'm just going to pull up another chair," Danny said, and my heart sank as Jon took the one across from me. I wanted to just get up and leave, but I knew that would draw too much attention.

"Anyone watch anything good on Netflix lately?"

Jon asked, and then laughed when they all just stared at him with varying shades of irritation.

The more Jon talked, the tighter my chest got. I kept swallowing like I had something stuck in my throat. Part of my mind was convinced I didn't have enough oxygen and would suffocate right here at the table. I pictured the horror and surprise on everyone's faces, the nurses running over to help. The more rational side of me knew that I could breathe fine, that this was only a panic attack.

What if he dies, though? I kept asking myself. *What if he dies like Amber and Katelyn?*

I risked a glance at him. He was laughing at something Danny had said, the emotion lighting up his face all the way to his eyes. He didn't look like someone who was suicidal—not that Katelyn ever had.

I knew what Dr. Williams or any other therapist would tell me to do: treat this as a delusional thought. But how could I do that when this was the third time I'd felt this way? This hot-cold, flu-like feeling. How could I not recognize it when it had just happened a few days ago before Katelyn died?

In the three days since her death, I had convinced myself I imagined it all, that maybe I just happened to have a panic attack and a weird dream before she died. But now that it was happening again, I had that bone-deep sense that something would happen to Jon.

I knew in the very core of me that he would die.

Group therapy with Julia again. Yesterday, I surprised myself by being able to at least tell the others how I felt, but I hadn't been in a constant state of panic. Now, all I could think about was Jon. How would it happen? Did he secretly feel suicidal like Katelyn? I doubted I would think about him this much if I had a thing for him.

"Sadie?" Julia asked, and I realized everyone was watching me. "Did you want to share today? You did so well yesterday."

I swallowed hard. *Do not say anything about Jon,* I warned myself. His name sat on the tip of my tongue, but I couldn't imagine how disturbed everyone would be if I just blurted out my worries.

"I'm still feeling anxious all the time," I said carefully. "I keep having nightmares, too."

Julia nodded as she wrote something on her notepad. "I'm sorry to hear that. Sometimes the nightmares can be the result of medication. Trazodone, for example, can cause vivid dreams and nightmares. Do you want to tell us about your dream? I'm no Carl Jung," she said with a grin, "but I may be able to help you make sense of it."

For a moment, I pictured myself describing my nightmare about Katelyn to the group. No doubt many of them had dreamed of her, too. It had been traumatic to hear about her killing herself. But I would have to say I dreamed of her death *before* she was found dead. What would they say? Who would even believe me?

Voices from my past whispered in my ears: *Crazy. Psycho. Overactive imagination.*

"No, that's okay," I said with another forced smile. "I can't really remember the details. I just know I'm having them because I wake up feeling panicked."

"That's not a fun way to wake up," Julia said sympathetically. "It might help to do a little bedtime meditation before you fall asleep. An easy one I like to do is to start with some square breathing—do y'all remember when we went over square breathing to manage anxiety?"

Everyone nodded, but I had no idea what she was talking about.

"What you do is breathe in deeply to the count of four, hold that breath to the count of four, let it out slowly to the count of four, and then repeat that four times." She drew a square in the air with her finger. "Four-four-four-four . . . a square. Get it?"

I nodded.

"The idea is to force you to take a moment and breathe slowly and deeply. Too many times we breathe shallowly, using our chests instead of our diaphragms." She demonstrated by taking quick, panting breaths. Her chest heaved. "Breathing with just your chest won't get you as much oxygen as breathing deeply, and oxygen can have a calming effect. Should we all try it? Everyone put your hand on your belly and blow it up like a big ol' beach ball."

Some of us cast embarrassed glances at each other, but most of us did as she asked. I noticed Aaron sat with his arms crossed though, like he didn't want to try it.

"Now, as you breathe in, you want to see your beach ball blow up. And when you breathe out, it will deflate again."

I did as she instructed, letting my eyes close. It seemed a little silly at first, but then I felt a sense of calm descend on me for the first time in days. I opened my eyes, but as soon as I saw Jon again, the same terrible feeling returned.

"Sadie, when you go to sleep tonight, I want you to try the square breathing, okay? But I want you to also picture yourself in the most relaxing setting you can. That might be the beach, or the mountains, or maybe even curled up by the fire with a book. Whatever you can think of that makes you feel calm and safe. Just picture it in your mind like a movie scene on repeat. Think you can try that tonight?"

"Okay," I told her, though it didn't seem likely to work. My imagination had always been the problem.

"Great," she said, beaming at me. "Let us know tomorrow if it worked for you. Aaron, would you like to share with us next?"

While Aaron spoke, I kept sneaking glances at Jon. He had a notebook in his lap that he used as a drawing pad. It looked like he was just doodling. If his painting in art was any indication, he wasn't the best artist. It seemed like he used it to keep his hands busy, since his foot constantly shook where he had it crossed at the ankle over his knee.

"I can't stop worrying about my friend," Aaron was saying, and when I glanced up, I saw him steal a glance at me. Was he talking about me? Or Jon? Did he sense something too?

Julia nodded and made a *hm* sound in the back of her throat. "That can be so hard, especially when you make friends here. I love that you care about each other—that's a good thing. But I want all of you to remember that you're here to work on yourselves, okay?"

She spent a moment eyeballing us and letting that sink in. "Everyone here is dealing with something, and let's be honest, if you're here, it's probably something pretty serious. Now imagine if each of you took on all of your friends' problems, too. You'd be too overwhelmed to function, let alone be able to address your own concerns.

"So let's all agree right now to stay in our own lanes and focus on our own stuff. If you're really worried about one thing in particular about your friend, then go to that friend and encourage them to talk to their therapist about it. Because you're here to support each other, but you don't have to take on the role of therapist, okay? That's what I'm here for."

She smiled and everyone nodded, including me, but inside, I didn't agree. I wasn't going to stay silent again when someone might die if I didn't try to help them.

"And what if that therapist fails to help and another one of us dies here?" Aaron asked, ropes of veins standing out on his arms as he gripped a notebook.

Julia tried to mask the surprised hurt, but I saw it flash across her face before she could. She didn't have as good of a poker face as Dr. Williams. "Are you talking about what happened to Katelyn, Aaron?"

"You know I am."

Tension mounted in the room. Julia looked sad. "Honestly, I struggle with what happened, too. That's the thing about suicide. It makes the survivors question what happened and play these horrible what-if games. What if I had just said this or done that? I don't know. That's the terrible part—I can't go back in time to see if she'd still be with us if I had just said the right thing. We all miss her, and we're all struggling with grief."

Aaron just looked down at the cover of his notebook silently.

He'd said what a lot of us had been thinking, though I didn't think Julia deserved to be called out like that.

"We can talk more about this after group if you'd like," she said.

"I'm good," he said without looking at her.

She watched him for a moment to see if he'd say

anything else, and when he didn't, she moved on. "Jon, did you want to share with us today?"

I tried not to act too interested, even though my whole body had stilled, waiting on his answer.

"I guess," he said, putting down his pen. "Things have been going better. I'm sleeping now."

Julia consulted her notes. "When you first came here, you hadn't slept in three days, right?"

"Yeah, I was so manic I was seeing and hearing things. That could have been the sleep loss, too."

"Have you had any manic symptoms lately?"

"Just racing thoughts, but I think that's how my brain works," he said with a grin.

"Racing thoughts aren't necessarily bad—it depends on how they affect you. What about depression? That's the flip-side of bipolar."

He shook his head. "I never really deal with depression. It's mostly mania, and even being locked up in this place for the last four months, I haven't had depressive symptoms. Well, not *many*," he amends with a sheepish look.

"This honestly isn't the worst place I've ever been," he continued. "I had to go to drug rehab for a while, and that was way worse. At least we have art therapy here. And people I can relate to."

I had to admit there was nothing about Jon's

words that would make me think he was suicidal. But then again, Katelyn never sounded like she wanted to hang herself. When I thought of the way she tried to comfort *me* after group the day before they found her dead, nausea rose fast and strong until I had to clench my teeth to keep it down.

As Julia talked about how helpful it could be to know others were struggling with the same problems, guilt gnawed at my insides. When I had the feeling that Amber would die, I hadn't said anything. When the same cold dread washed over me about Katelyn, I didn't say a word either, even when I had plenty of opportunity to talk to her. I would have to be a sociopath not to do something this time.

I willed Julia to ask him more about his depressive thoughts—like, when was the last time he had any?—but she'd already moved on.

For the rest of group, I kept sneaking glances at Jon, as if he would suddenly give some kind of sign. He went back to doodling, his foot still bouncing like he had excess energy. We would all go to rec next, so I would have an opportunity to talk to him then. I knew I would struggle to say something because I generally avoided confrontation at all costs. Any threat of argument made me want to tug a hooded sweatshirt over my head and hide, but these stupid scrubs we wore didn't even give us that luxury.

The thought of Jon killing himself made me willing to endure it if it would keep him alive.

The second group ended, I hurried over to Jon in a rush and said, "Hey, do you think we could talk for a minute when we go to rec?"

He raised his eyebrows at me, and I could tell I had spent way too much time in my own head and come on a little strong. He glanced at Aaron before answering me. "Uh, I would, but I'm meeting with Dr. Williams during rec today."

All the determination I had talked myself into deflated like a popped balloon. I had been so ready to wring the truth out of him, and now I would have to wait for some other time. Already my palms were sweating with anxiety at the prospect of having to wait and worry for the rest of the day.

"I'm sure I'll see you at dinner, though," he said. "Maybe we can talk then?"

He still looked like maybe that was the last thing he wanted to do, especially when I blurted out an overly enthusiastic agreement.

He and Aaron gave me one more concerned glance before leaving, but I couldn't let it bother me.

I would rather they think I was acting crazy than live with the guilt of another death.

Now I would just have to think of some way to convince Jon to tell me how he's been feeling.

Should be super easy considering we've shared maybe two conversations the whole time I've been here, I thought with an inward eye roll. But I was willing to endure the awkwardness if it meant helping him.

After dinner, I finally had my chance to corner Jon. He had been sitting with Danny and Aaron while Becca, Millie, and I were at another table. As soon as he stood to put his tray away, I jumped up to do the same.

"Hey," I said to him when we were out of earshot of everyone else. "Can we talk for a second now?"

Jon looked resigned, but he nodded. We moved to a relatively quiet area of the room. Out of the corner of my eye, I could tell our friends kept sneaking glances at us. It made things about ten times more awkward. My face grew hot, flushing from a combination of embarrassment and nerves.

"What's up, Sadie?" Jon asked, arms crossed over his chest.

I tried not to let his obvious discomfort bother me. "This is going to sound like it's coming out of the blue, but after everything that happened here with Katelyn, I feel like it would be wrong if I didn't ask questions."

His brows knitted even more. "What are you talking about?"

"I just get this . . . sense that maybe you're having a harder time than you're saying. Like maybe you're struggling with depression."

He looked taken aback. "You think I'm depressed?"

"It's more like I'm afraid you're hiding being depressed. Like, I know you said during group that you mostly deal with mania, but you also said you sometimes have depressive thoughts."

The look he gave me was honestly like I had sprouted horns. "Why are you trying to be a shrink? What do you care if I'm depressed or not?"

I tried not to bristle at his tone, but I could feel my blush spread down my neck. "I told you why I care—I don't want the same thing to happen to you that happened to Katelyn."

"Okay, well, I'm not suicidal, so I don't see how

I'm going to end up hanging myself from the ceiling."

"I just really don't want anything to happen to you."

His eyes widened at that, and his tone softened when he answered. "I appreciate that, Sadie, but just so you know, I kinda have something going with Danny."

It took me a full ten seconds to realize what he was getting at. "Oh! No, that's not what this is about—"

He reached out and touched my shoulder. "I'll be sure to let you know if I start feeling like I might off myself, okay?"

His tone held a note of condescension, but I couldn't let it get to me. I couldn't just give up.

"Don't make us all find you like that. Think of the way Danny reacted to losing Katelyn. She was his friend, but if y'all are together, then I can't imagine how upset he'll be, or what he'll do."

His expression twisted into annoyance. "Thanks for putting that image in my head. I don't know how many ways I can tell you I'm not suicidal before you believe me, so I think I'm just going to walk away. I'll see you later."

I watched him leave, my whole body drenched in

that hot-cold feeling, causing sweat to track down my spine. I had embarrassed myself and made us both uncomfortable, and I didn't even know if it was worth it. Would a suicidal person even admit they felt that way? I could only hope he'd think twice about it now that I had pointed out how devastated Danny would be.

I just didn't want to wake up to find someone else had killed themselves in this place.

11

That same night, I hesitated at the fork in the hallway that led to the boys' side of the house. We weren't allowed to go in their rooms, but the temptation to sneak down there anyway grabbed hold of me. Maybe Jon had been guarded talking to me after dinner. I was annoyed at myself for pushing him. When I started thinking and worrying about something, the obsession became like a leech that latched onto my mind and wouldn't let go. The only way to make the knots in my stomach disappear was to do something about it. So I had. I had pushed him to talk to me, and all it had done was make him think I was suddenly into him.

The mental health aides tended to patrol the floors around bedtime because they wanted us safely in our beds so they could zone out and stare at their phones. One of the girls had already been caught sneaking down the boys' hallway multiple times this week and sent back to her room. Apparently, she suffered from a psychotic disorder that made her hypersexual. Hooking up at a mental facility was generally frowned upon since we were all dealing with some heavy stuff. So, they definitely didn't want us going into bedrooms with someone of the opposite sex.

I glanced down the hall but didn't see any of the aides. I only had to think of tossing and turning endlessly in my bed, stomach churning, to decide I was willing to risk it.

I hurried along, staying by the ugly puce walls and scanning the names outside the doors as I went. Then it hit me: Jon was Aaron's roommate. Aaron would most likely be in the room with him right now. I thought of all the times I'd caught Aaron watching me, of his concern for me and kind eyes. And now I planned to have another awkward conversation with Jon where he would undoubtedly decide for good that I was out of my mind.

But there was something about being in your own space, away from others, that made you more open to sharing and being vulnerable. Maybe in his own room, Jon would tell me the truth about his feelings. Aaron might even help get him to open up, especially after he'd freaked out on Julia in group. Surely if he thought his roommate might kill himself, he'd help me stop him, right?

I had just made it to the sixth door when a gruff voice called out to me. "Sadie, what are you doing in the boys' hall?"

I turned to find one of the aides, Jax, glowering at me, his beefy arms crossed over his chest. I recognized him as the one they called when they needed an aide to manhandle one of the patients. He looked more like a bouncer than someone who worked in a mental health facility, with a shaved head and tree trunks for legs. He cocked his head at me, and even his neck looked thick. A little shiver of unease went down my spine.

"Oh," I said, pretending to look around in confusion, "I didn't realize I went down the wrong hall."

He just kept staring at me like he didn't believe a single word of that. "It's past bedtime, so head back to your room now."

I nodded and turned back for the hallway entrance, my stomach in knots. Maybe I could come later and try to talk to Jon.

I had just made it past Jax's bulk when he added,

"And Sadie? I'll be walking this hallway all night, so make sure you don't get confused again."

"I won't," I mumbled, hating that he had seemingly read my mind.

I just hoped we wouldn't all wake up to find Jon dead in the morning.

***

The nightmare sank claws of fear in me, making it impossible to escape. I had tried the square breathing and meditation Julia suggested, but I still tossed and turned for what felt like hours. And then I had fallen into a shadowy dream that refused my every attempt to change it. Helplessly, I stood in Aaron and Jon's room. They slept with their beds across from one another, each against the wall of their boxy space. Aaron slept on his back, one arm over his eyes as he snored lightly. But the dream wasn't focused on him.

It was focused on the figure standing over Jon as he slept.

Just like in the last nightmare, I could see through the killer's eyes and look down on his sleeping form. Jon slept on his back, one arm behind his head. His heavy breaths continued despite the threat hovering over him.

The killer leaned toward him, something sharp glinting in the dim light. I couldn't tell what he held, but I knew it was deadly.

No, I tried to scream, but in that way of dreams, no sound escaped. Like I was trapped behind glass, able to see what was happening but powerless to stop it.

Before the killer could do anything, a furtive sound came from behind them. They whipped around toward the door.

A small, mousey girl slipped into the room. When I recognized Millie, I tried to scream a warning to her.

Millie, run! I thought, but again, no sound escaped.

The killer didn't hesitate. They stalked toward Millie, backing her into a wall. Her eyes were huge as her mouth opened in a silent scream. She raised her hands protectively in front of herself.

Behind my glass, I screamed and begged for them to leave her alone.

The killer leaned toward Millie threateningly.

And then I woke up.

The only sound I could hear was my heartbeat, crashing loudly against my ribcage. The dream had seemed as painfully real as the one I had before Katelyn died. Only Millie hadn't been in that one.

I jerked my head toward her side of the room, but I could see her bed was empty. My heart sank like a rock in deep water.

"Millie?" I called as I got out of bed. But there was no response. She wasn't here.

What if the killer got to her, too?

Goosebumps broke over my skin as I hurriedly put on shoes and left our room.

I checked the bathroom but didn't find her there. A voice in my mind whispered I would never find her because she and Jon were already gone. I had failed to warn him, and somehow Millie got wrapped up in the whole thing.

My shoes made heavy thumping sounds as I raced down the stairs. Usually at this time, they both were at breakfast, so I completely ignored the line to get my morning meds. A nurse shouted at me when I ran by. I only had a few minutes before they sicked an aide on me.

I stood in the entrance of the dining room, my gaze darting from table to table. A horrible mantra repeated in my head: *they're dead. They're both dead.*

A chuckle came from a table near the back, and that's when I saw him. Jon. Alive and well with Danny beside him.

I stared at him uncomprehendingly.

Had the killer been thwarted by Millie?

I swung my head to look for her, part of me still believing she wouldn't be there. But then I saw her, having just thrown away her trash and replaced her tray.

Before I could even process what I was seeing, I hurried over to her and grabbed her arm. "Millie, are you okay? What happened last night?" I demanded in a harsh whisper.

She responded by widening her eyes like saucers and shaking her head.

"Were you in Jon's room, too? Did you see anything?" The questions just tumbled out of my mouth even though I knew she wouldn't be able to answer me. The need for the truth about my dream clawed at my mind like a caged animal.

I must have been gripping poor Millie's arm too hard in my desperation because she jerked it away from me and clutched it to herself.

"I know you don't talk, but just nod once if you were in his room. If you saw what I saw." I had moved so close to her that we were only a few inches from each other. Tears swam in her eyes.

Suddenly, she shoved me back and whirled away at the same time. She practically ran down the hall to escape from me.

That's when I turned to find Jax watching me. "Sadie, is there something going on with you and Millie?" he asked.

I knew what Jax being there meant. Not only had I missed meds, but they'd called him because the nursing staff thought I was losing it. He was the one strong enough to haul me to Dr. Williams.

When I focused on Jax, looming over me in a semi-threatening way, I realized the whole room had been staring at me. No one had missed the exchange I had with Millie.

A scream built inside me, but I swallowed it down.

They all thought I was crazy.

Maybe you are, a voice said inside me.

I didn't answer Jax because I couldn't. I ducked my head and left the dining room. I fast-walked over to the nurse's med station and held my hand out for my little cup of pills.

"You're playing with fire not coming to get your meds first thing like you're supposed to, Sadie," Nurse Jackie said with a scowl. She practically crushed the cup into my hand.

I ignored her as I cheeked the antipsychotic and swallowed the other two.

When no one could see me anymore, I ran to my room. I burst through the door and let out a breath in relief that poor Millie wasn't in here. My cheeks flamed at the memory of yelling at her like that. No wonder she'd looked so afraid.

I crawled into bed and covered my head with the thin blanket. I tried the square breathing technique. In for four . . . out for four . . . but then I'd lose track. I couldn't escape my thoughts. All along, I'd believed that I had prophetic dreams, that I knew when someone was about to die. But Jon had been one of the kids staring at me while I shook Millie down like a loan shark. He was perfectly fine. Nothing had happened to Millie either, even after I clearly saw her being threatened by the killer in my dream. And Katelyn hadn't died the way I dreamed either. Had I even dreamed her death before it happened? Maybe I just thought I did, but it had all been a fantasy made up in my mind.

Otherwise known as psychosis.

They said if you were truly insane you never questioned your sanity, and maybe that was what happened to me.

Because there was only one conclusion I could come to now that Jon and Millie were alive and well:

It was all in my head.

12

———

I almost didn't go to group after that. The realization that my dream was only a figment of my unhinged mind weighed on me so heavily that I continued to hide all morning in my room. I couldn't face everyone else after I acted like that to Millie. I would have stayed there all day if Becca hadn't come to find me.

"You coming to group?" she asked as I lay in my bed facing away from her.

"No."

"Why not?"

I squeezed my eyes shut against the images of what happened in the dining room this morning. "Because I'm wallowing in my humiliation."

She made a *tsk*-ing sound. "You think you're the

only one who's lost it in front of everyone in this place? Girl, get over yourself."

I rolled over to look at her. "Someone sicked Jax on me."

"Yeah, maybe, but you're not the only one that's ever happened to. In case you haven't noticed, someone has a breakdown or freaks out here every day. It's why we're in a mental hospital."

I thought back to that first morning here when one of the girls got hauled away like an animal at the zoo. Everyone in the dining room had barely stopped what they were doing to watch, like it was no big deal. I supposed yelling at Millie like a psychopath paled in comparison.

Becca must have seen that I was softening because she reached out and touched my shoulder. "The whole point of all this therapy is to talk it out. We all get it. No judgments—really. Millie is probably even ready to forgive and forget, and you yelled at her like a psycho." I glanced at her face to see if she was seriously calling me that, but her teasing smirk let me know how she really felt.

So I got up and made it to group. Now I sat here, half-listening to everyone do their feelings check-in, sweating at the thought of telling everyone how I felt.

I thought about the icy-cold sensation I'd had about Katelyn and Jon. Had I completely misread all my feelings? Before Amber and Katelyn died, I didn't just have the horrible sensation like someone was walking over my grave, but also dreams of their deaths. But the mind was a tricky thing. What if I just thought I had those dreams? What if it was all my imagination the next day?

Once I read an article about how there were people who could never remember their dreams. How they'd struggle to hold onto the wisp of dream memory, but it would slip through their fingers like fog the moment they completely woke up. The nightmares I had about Katelyn, Jon, and Amber had been so vivid, so detailed. They were more like traumatic memories than dreams.

In Katelyn's case, this made even more sense. I dreamed she was killed in her bed, not hanged. But even when I was presented with the proof—that my nightmare hadn't been accurate—I still believed I had psychic powers. When I was little, my parents and teachers encouraged fantasies like this. I made comic books and elaborate stories, drawings and art. But as I got older, the shrinks began calling my imagination by a new name: delusions.

Delusions were like getting lost in your own

dreamworld and forgetting it wasn't reality. When you start to believe it's all real, that's when all the therapists accuse you of being psychotic.

The mind is a powerful thing, and I had no doubt I was capable of tricking myself into believing I had some sort of superpower.

Because what was the alternative? That I was crazy and belonged in a mental hospital?

I swallowed the lump in my throat. Obviously, that was the truth, and it was time to admit it.

After taking a deep breath, I raised my hand.

Julia's slightly bushy eyebrows shot into her hairline. "Sadie? Did you want to share something with us?"

"I think—" I began, and then immediately had to clear my throat to hide the waver in my voice. I tried again. "I think I'm ready to admit I have a problem. I'm not okay, and I think I need to be here."

"That is so brave of you," Julia said in a gentle tone. "Was there anything that made you come to that conclusion?"

I couldn't help but glance over at Jon. He wasn't watching me—Aaron was. My face flushed. "I just realized that I've been believing my own delusions. It sounds silly saying it out loud, but I had convinced myself I had this superpower, like I was starring in a Marvel movie or something." I let out a weak laugh. "I'm just figuring out that it was complete make-believe."

I had my shoulders hunched around my ears, waiting for everyone to start laughing at me. Instead, many of them nodded. Like succumbing to self-deception was a relatable thing. And I guess it was—in a mental hospital.

Becca reached over and squeezed my hand, and when I looked up, everyone was nodding at me encouragingly.

"Acknowledging delusional thoughts is the first step to learning to manage them effectively," Julia said. "In fact, many people suffer from problematic thinking that's just one step away from delusions. We call this type of negative thinking 'cognitive distortions,' but that's just a fancy way of saying, 'twisted thinking.'

"One example that I know everyone—including me—has experienced is jumping to conclusions. Have you ever thought someone was mad at you just because they looked upset, and then later you found out the real reason had nothing to do with you? That's an example of twisted thinking. You thought you could read their mind."

It was funny that Julia chose jumping to conclusions as her example, since that's exactly what I had done with my dreams. It felt like a weight rolled off my shoulders when I saw the others nodding, too. Maybe I wasn't the only one here who had thought they were some kind of mind reader.

"I'll give all of you a handout on the list of common cognitive distortions at the end of group," Julia was saying to the others before turning back to me. "And thank you so much for sharing with us today, Sadie."

When group ended, Aaron came over to me, his warm eyes holding mine. I knew the others had warned me against him, but there was something about Aaron that made me feel safe, like he truly cared about me. Which I knew could be another fantasy since he didn't even really know me. He was just one of those people who put me at ease. "That must have been really hard for you to talk about, so I just wanted to tell you that you aren't alone."

"It was pretty embarrassing to admit, so I appreciate you saying that."

Aaron glanced back to where Jon, Danny, and Becca were talking. Danny and Jon were joking with each other, but Becca was watching me with disapproval written all over her face. I lifted my brows slightly in a silent question, but she just shook her head.

"I'm constantly fighting my own thoughts, too, so I could relate." He leaned a little closer. "I have to admit, I was low-key worried you would say you were into Jon and upset he didn't reciprocate. I was a little relieved when you described your thoughts as something totally different."

I groaned and shook my head. "Unrequited love would have been more normal, I think. I already regret telling the group my stupid delusions of having superhero powers. Like, what am I, five?"

He laughed. "Don't you know that delusions of grandeur are the best kind? That's how you convince yourself you're the King of England and shit."

"More like Professor X, but okay," I said with a grin.

"*X-Men*, huh? Nice. I could get on board with that. I always did have a thing for Rogue."

He held my gaze while we smiled at each other, and my heart leaped in my chest.

"Sadie!" Becca's voice cut in. I looked up to find her still waiting by the door. "Come on. We're going to miss lunch."

"Oh good, wouldn't want to miss out on meat-loaf, or glue passing as mashed potatoes, or whatever other culinary atrocities they have planned for us today," I said with an eye roll before turning back to Aaron. "You coming?"

He shook his head. "It's my turn with Dr. Williams, so I'll have to eat my gluey mashed potatoes later."

I made a face. "Hopefully they'll at least warm them up for you."

He smiled. "If I'm lucky. I'll see you later," he said and touched my shoulder. Warmth shot through me at the brief connection, and I tried to ignore the butterflies in my stomach. *Get it together, Sadie.*

As soon as he left and I joined Danny and Becca, Danny waggled his eyebrows at me. "I couldn't help but notice you and Aaron staring into each other's eyes and grinning like idiots for five awkward minutes."

I let out a surprised laugh. "It was like five seconds—max."

"That's not what I saw," Danny said, still with a suggestive expression on his face.

Becca fake-gagged as we made our way to the dining room to get lunch. I could smell that it was something horrible. Possibly broccoli. Hopefully there would at least be a roll I could choke down.

"Don't encourage it," Becca said with her arms

crossed over her chest. "That's the last thing any of us needs to focus on, honestly. We need to just work on ourselves and get the hell out of here."

Danny let out an exaggerated groan. "Don't listen to this Basic Betty. She clearly hates all kinds of fun and happiness. I guess it hasn't occurred to her that having a little innocent side action here might actually help your mood improve, but whatever."

"Like we need to be messing with relationships right now—that all went *so* well on the outside," she countered, holding up her hand when Danny tried to argue. "But Aaron in particular weirds me out."

"I don't get that," I told her.

"Yeah, Jon says he's a nice guy," Danny said. "And as his roommate, I feel like he would know."

"He's just always staring at you like he's obsessed or something," Becca said to me with a shake of her head. "Like go away, focus on your own shit."

"Maybe I don't mind him staring at me," I said, and Danny snickered.

Becca gave me a hard look, but Danny threw one arm around me. "This is a girl after my own heart. I'm in a fucking mental hospital, but I still have to have something fun to distract myself with."

"Speaking of Jon," I said with a laugh when Danny raised his eyebrows at me, "I bet he told you how I totally embarrassed myself and made him think I was hitting on him."

Danny nodded with faux sadness as we all sat down at one of the round tables. "Yes, I had to hear way too much about that. Jon was convinced his teasing had made you think he was into you. Which, I told him that you clearly didn't know about us because *obviously* he would prefer me over you. No offense."

Honestly, I was kind of relieved about that. Maybe now he wouldn't ridicule my paintings during art or call me darkness. One small positive of this whole mess.

"You're right, I didn't realize that about the two of you, but I definitely wasn't trying to hit on him, anyway."

"What were you trying to do?" Becca asked with genuine curiosity as she slathered her roll with a pat of butter.

There was no way I wanted to admit to my friends that I had convinced myself I could predict someone's imminent death, so I decided to stick to a half-truth. "That was part of my self-deception, apparently. I thought I was picking up on depression and suicidal thoughts in Jon that no one else knew about. Like I was some sort of super shrink," I said with a soft laugh.

"I could have told you he was fine," Danny said, but his grin faded when he added, "although, I thought Katelyn was fine, too." He teared up and had to take a steadying breath.

"That was what I thought, too," I said. "I guess I was just scared of something like that happening again."

"We get it," Becca said with a nod. "That's why I told you not to worry about being judged here. We've all dealt with obsessive thoughts or just crazy thinking."

"Before I came here, I had to count to twenty-six before I did anything, or I was sure my mom would die," Danny said. "It sounds ridiculous and insane now, and I knew it was before, but I couldn't stop. If I got interrupted, I had to start all over. There was one time during a test that the teacher failed me because I got up to go to the bathroom, counting in my head, but she interrupted me, so I had to start all over. It took me so long to even get to the classroom door that she thought I was cheating and failed me."

"OCD is no joke," Becca agreed.

I wasn't sure OCD was what I was dealing with —if it was, the shrinks never told me. But it still made me feel better to hear that my friends dealt with weird mental health stuff too.

And for the first time, I thought maybe I could let myself open up and be vulnerable.

Maybe then I could figure out the truth about the way my mind worked.

D r. Williams's office was as unwelcoming as ever. Same ugly artwork. Same tired old couch. Instead of letting it pull my mood down until it spiraled into something closely resembling depression, I focused on the fact that I finally held the key to getting out of here: accepting that I had fantasies I tricked myself into believing, and I needed to work on not doing that anymore.

Dr. Williams crossed his legs and set his notepad on his knee. He wore his usual uniform of khaki pants and a boring button-down shirt. "I understand you had a real breakthrough during group today. Dr. Mendez made a note of it in your chart," he added when I glanced up in surprise.

"Yeah, I didn't tell the group the whole story because it sounds too crazy, but I think I'm ready to tell you."

His usually sleepy-looking eyes brightened with interest behind his glasses. "I would like that, Sadie."

I avoided looking at him and focused on the view out the window instead. "I told you before that I had a dream my sister would die before she did and that I got that awful feeling, but what I didn't tell you is that the same thing happened with Katelyn. Or, at least, I thought it did."

He made a *hm* sound to show he was listening, so I forged ahead.

"The day before Katelyn died, I had the same terrible feeling I had before Amber died in the fire. I felt hot and cold and panicky. I could barely catch my breath, and I had to go someplace quiet to calm down. And then, the morning Katelyn died, I woke up and remembered this horrible dream of her dying."

Something crossed his face so fast I couldn't register what it was. "All of that must have been very distressing. So every time someone you know or love dies, you remember having a dream about their death?"

"Yes. And when the same thing happened with Jon—same sensation and a horrible dream—I was convinced he was going to die."

Dr. Williams tapped his chin with his pen. "As far

as your symptoms go, it sounds like you're describing panic attacks."

I nodded. "It definitely felt like a panic attack, just really intense. When I saw that Jon was fine after I had that same feeling and dream, I started to wonder if I had been delusional all along. Like maybe I didn't even have the dreams—I just thought I did. And that's when I realized that I really do need to be here."

"And just to be clear: you're saying you may have remembered the dream only after discovering what had happened to Amber and Katelyn?"

Hearing my sister's name brought a shot of pain to my heart, but I tried to focus on his question. "Yes, like maybe I just convinced myself I had the dream before I found out what had happened to them. While in reality my mind made it all up."

He considered that for a moment. "Delusions can be very powerful. What do you think was the purpose of all this self-deception?"

"I think I wanted to feel powerful," I said, heat blooming across my cheeks. "Like I had some magical gift instead of just being mentally ill."

"That's a very plausible explanation, though I think there's another component to it. In the case of your sister, I think your mind was trying to shield you from the terrible loss by giving you something else to focus on. As bad as guilt feels, it's an emotion we're all familiar with. Sometimes our minds would rather deal with guilt than grief."

"I don't know. Feeling guilty really sucks, too."

"I can't argue with that, but I suppose with our subconscious, it prefers the devil it knows. In your case, you made yourself feel responsible for these untimely deaths because you thought you had predicted them. I'm sorry you put yourself through that, Sadie."

I rubbed my arms. "I still feel bad, even though I know I couldn't have done anything to stop them dying. I still can't shake that feeling."

He nodded again. "I think you're going to feel that way for a while because you're not quite ready to face your sister's death. Maybe Katelyn's death, too." Images of the fire threatened at the edges of my mind, my nostrils starting to detect the acrid smell of smoke, but I tamped it down. "I'm so proud of you, though, for realizing that you need to work on these distorted thoughts and delusions so you can start to feel better."

I looked up at him. "And get out of here?"

"You've taken the first step to being able to leave. You've acknowledged that you've been suffering from delusions. Now we must begin the work to help you learn to confront those distorted thought patterns."

I swallowed hard. "That sounds like it will take a long time. How much longer am I going to be in here?"

He leveled his gaze at me. "As long as it takes."

I didn't like the sound of that. I saw the months stretching out in front of me, friends leaving while I was still trapped here.

And what about my family? They abandoned me here, and for what? Distorted thoughts and dreams?

I struggled to picture the day my parents brought me here, the car trip and the events that led up to it. But where the memories should be, an impenetrable mental block loomed.

For now, I retreated from the wall in my mind. My past and everything that transpired before I came to this horrible place was behind it, but I didn't want to tear down the wall.

I may have been ready to acknowledge that I wasn't one hundred percent mentally well, but I knew I wasn't prepared to face everything that had happened in my past.

Not yet.

13

Millie and I may have been roommates, but somehow she still managed to avoid me ever since I'd lost it on her in the dining room. For the past two nights, I'd tried to talk to her before going to bed, but it was like she anticipated the earliest I could get to our room. It seemed like every night she was asleep in her bed by eight. Or at least was pretending to be. She lay in bed so quietly I couldn't tell for sure if she was faking it or not. Never talking or laughing made it easy to fake me out.

When I walked into art therapy that afternoon and saw an open seat next to Millie, a rush of determination filled me. I would apologize and make it right.

Instead of the easels and paint set up like last time, each paint-stained table contained sketchbooks and drawing supplies. The charcoal pencils were not as nice a brand as the ones I had at home, but I still itched to use them. Nothing soothed my overanxious mind as much as art.

I sat down beside Millie, and her shoulders stiffened like she expected me to say something right away. So I didn't. Usually, I couldn't stand to be patient, but just the thought of being able to sketch relaxed me.

Shandra's messy hair was paint-flecked again today and held back with a scarf away from her face. She greeted us with a warm smile.

After the usual hello and feelings check-in, she explained what we would be doing with the sketchbooks today.

"We focus a lot on the positive in therapy, which is important, but we also don't want to discount the very real demons that you struggle with on a daily basis." She walked over to one of the tables and picked up an art pad.

"Each of you has a sketchbook and charcoal pencils to draw with. What I want you to focus on today are those inner demons that torment you. The anxiety, anger, sadness, repetitive thoughts—I want you to bring them to life on the page. The best way to confront your fears and problems is to drag them into the light, so that's what we're going to do in our art."

She put the blank sketchbook down and walked over to a table that held art from past sessions. After sifting through a pile of sketches, she held up one for us to look at. The detail on it captivated me. The artist had layered multiple faces on top of each other while keeping them distinct. At first, it appeared they were different people, but then I realized the artist had drawn the same girl wearing different expressions. One was sorrowful, another was twisted with rage, and yet another was wide-eyed with terror. It brought a chill across my skin to look at, but at the same time, I couldn't tear my eyes away.

"This was done by a very talented patient, as you can see," Shandra said with a hint of pride as she looked at the picture. "She chose to illustrate the many different emotions that she struggled with. Yours doesn't have to be this detailed. It could be a simple black cloud hovering over you, or maybe a hole in the ground to symbolize how depression often makes us feel like it's impossible to dig out of."

She gave a few more examples, but I returned my attention to the first sketch. The bottom right-hand corner drew my gaze, and I read the signature written there. Surprise shot through me when I saw it said Lisa. This girl again. The mystery continued. Every time I forgot about her and focused on something else, it seemed like her name came up again. Whoever she was, she had incredible artistic talent. I glanced at the dark sketch, at the rage so clearly expressed on one of the faces, and cringed. Talented and disturbed.

"Go ahead and get started," Shandra was saying, "and I'll be around to help as needed."

A flurry of noise and activity filled the room as everyone sorted through the supplies on the tables and settled into drawing. Millie stayed quiet as usual, reaching for the pack of charcoal pencils closest to her. I stared at my blank page, waiting for inspiration to strike. What I really wanted to do was talk to Millie, though.

"Millie?" I tried, but she kept drawing and didn't glance my way. "Can I talk to you about something for a second?"

Still nothing.

Millie took the silent treatment to a whole new level. I watched her sketch slowly and deliberately for a little while, trying to figure out how I could get her to listen to me. Suddenly, her elbow accidentally bumped into one of the pencils and knocked it to the floor. She reached to get it, but I picked it up first.

She frowned at me with a heavy dose of suspicion in her eyes.

Handing it to her with a sheepish smile, I quietly said, "Millie, I'm so sorry I yelled at you like that the other day."

Her eyes dropped to the floor, but she didn't turn back to her drawing, so I knew she was listening, at least.

"I didn't mean to scare you. I just got all caught up in these crazy obsessive thoughts I was having, and I think I took it out on you. I had this vivid dream with you in it," I said with a shake of my head. "I convinced myself it was real."

She still didn't look at me, and my heart twisted. She reminded me of a puppy who expected to be hit as often as it was petted.

"I would never hurt you, Millie," I said with all the sincerity I could convey. I reached out and touched her arm gently.

Slowly, she raised her head so that our eyes met.

Encouraged, I pressed on. "I'm really working on those obsessive thoughts now, and I swear I'll never yell at you like that again. Can you forgive me?"

She kept her head down, but then all of a

sudden, she leaned toward me and gave me a quick hug. Before I could even pat her back in response, she pulled away and resumed her drawing.

I returned to my own sketch with a smile on my face. I felt so much lighter, it was hard to focus on the assignment.

While my mind wandered, my fingers grabbed hold of the charcoal and sketched. I thought of my anxiety, which seemed to guide my every decision lately. If I didn't do what my thoughts told me to, my anxiety ramped up to the point where my chest felt so tight I couldn't breathe.

I drew a girl like me, bent over with her hands on either side of her head. She clutched her hair, but where her head should be, there was only a black mass of jagged lines. I blurred the very center of the blackness, symbolizing the dark hole at the center of my thoughts.

"That's very good, Sadie," Shandra said from behind me.

I turned back and flashed a smile at her. "Thank you. It's supposed to be my anxiety." She pointed to the mass of jagged lines. "I think this represents the chaotic feeling of anxiety really well."

Her attention shifted to Millie's drawing. "I like yours, too, Millie. Does this figure represent some sort of fear you deal with? They look like they're standing over the bed threateningly."

Millie nodded slowly, and that was when I got a good look at the sketch. I froze in my seat.

She had drawn a shadowed figure hovering threateningly over someone in bed. Someone that looked a lot like Jon.

I searched Millie's face, but she gave nothing away.

Don't get caught up in your delusions again, I told myself.

But it was so hard when it looked like my room-mate had drawn a scene from my dream.

As I walked down the hall from art therapy, I tried to convince myself that Millie's drawing wasn't the big deal I thought it was. It could be the whole "jumping to conclusions" thing that Julia had talked about in group. For one thing, the drawing looked like any of the rooms here. They were all boxy with two twin beds. And honestly, Millie wasn't the best artist. What I took for a boy with short, tousled hair like Jon's could have been anyone. The shadowy figure standing over the bed creeped me out because it resembled the scene from my dream, but even something like that wasn't unique. Shandra asked us to draw our fears and struggles, and Millie's sketch looked like a nightmare brought to life. I just wasn't sure whose nightmare.

I got so wrapped up in my own thoughts that I almost walked right past Aaron.

He sat on the bottom steps of the back staircase, head in his hands. We may have been in a mental institution, but I had gotten used to Aaron being pretty even-tempered. Well, except for that time he got mad at Julia during group. I hadn't seen this sorrowful side of him yet, and it made my heart twist.

"Aaron?" I said tentatively. "Are you okay?"

At the sound of my voice, his hands dropped down, and he lifted his head. His eyes looked shadowed.

"I've been better," he said with a sad smile.

I sat beside him on the stairs. "Did something happen?"

He swiped a hand over his face and groaned. "I just got out of a session with Dr. Williams. I thought he would say I was finally ready to go home. I've been doing much better, and it's already been months. If he's waiting until I'm 100 percent better, I don't think that's ever going to happen."

"I get it. I may not have been here long, but I'm already desperate to leave. He won't even give me a timeline."

"Yeah, that's what he does. It just feels like everyone leaves me behind—and not just here. My dad, my brother. They left without a backward glance."

"I'm sorry," I said, thinking of how I had lost my own sister. "It must have been awful losing your brother and your dad."

He scoffed. "I didn't lose anyone. My dad bailed the second a psychiatrist diagnosed me, and my brother joined the army the day after he graduated high school. I haven't talked to him since."

I thought of how kind Aaron had always been to me, and I couldn't imagine his own family just leaving him like that. "That sucks, Aaron. You don't deserve it."

"Thanks," he said heavily. "And it's hard here, too. It's like a revolving door. I mean, it should be because that means kids are getting better and leaving, but it's still hard to watch. It feels like getting left all over again. First it was my friend Matt, and then Lisa."

I glanced up at the mention of her name. "I saw her sketch today in art therapy—it was amazing."

He gave me sort of a strange, confused look. "Oh, you mean a drawing she left behind. Yeah, she's an incredible artist." Before I could even attempt to awkwardly ask about her, he continued. "Now Jon's supposed to be leaving soon. He even came here after I did. I'm happy for him, don't get me wrong, but it's just another reminder that I'm still stuck here while everyone else gets to move on with life. I must have that Stockholm Syndrome or whatever because part of me doesn't even want to leave—how messed up is that?"

I didn't know what to say that would make him feel better, because honestly, his situation did suck. Mine sucked, too. I wanted so badly to ask about Lisa, but I didn't think he would want to talk about her right now. I reached out and took his hand. It was warm and strong. I gave it a squeeze and hoped it conveyed something meaningful and comforting. Something beyond words.

He looked at me in surprise for a moment but then ended up squeezing my hand back gently.

That night, Millie smiled at me before getting into bed. After so many nights of her completely avoiding me, it felt like a huge step. I lay in bed and told myself that now I would be able to sleep with zero worries. We had moved past me acting like a psycho in front of everyone in the dining room, and now maybe things could go back to normal—whatever that was in a mental hospital.

But as usual, my mind wouldn't turn off.

It jumped from the creepy sketch of faces Lisa drew to Millie's weird drawing. Why was it so much like my dream? Had Millie been there in Jon's room? Was that real?

No, I thought, squeezing my eyes shut tight. *Don't go down this road again.*

If you knew you had deceptive thoughts, then how could you trust your own mind? Your own thoughts and feelings? What I thought I had dreamed couldn't be trusted either. And suddenly, the thought of sleeping and dreaming had my intestines knotting inside me. All the creepy sketches and thoughts I had would probably lead to a nightmare, and then I would wake up more confused than ever.

I tossed and turned for a few minutes before finally giving up and grabbing an old, beat up paperback I'd found during rec. I went over to the door of our room and sat down cross-legged on the floor. Weak yellow light came from underneath the door, and I used it to illuminate the pages of my book.

It was going to be a long night.

14

Usually, I only drank coffee if it had a ratio of something like ninety percent creamer and ten percent coffee. Coffee always had a nasty, bitter aftertaste to me. But after a night spent not sleeping, I could endure a little bitterness if it would clear up the fog that had descended in my mind.

I had gone to breakfast the second I could at seven in the morning while everyone else with sense slept peacefully in their beds. The dining room stood practically empty. As I ripped open and spilled my third packet of sugar, I realized staying up all night again might send me over the edge. I really didn't want to talk to Dr. Williams about it, but maybe he could give me something that would prevent nightmares.

I was debating whether to go to his office now or wait until after morning group when Aaron walked in, looking just as groggy as I felt. I waved him over after he got his breakfast tray. He sat down heavily.

"Did you pull an all-nighter, too?" I asked with a nod toward the steaming cup of black coffee on his tray.

"Just my usual racing thoughts keeping me up." He pointed to my cup. "What about you?"

"Same," I said, not wanting to admit that I had been worried about dreams leading to more delusional thinking.

"I'm actually glad you're out here alone," he said, then shook his head. "Sorry, that came out wrong. I meant so I could thank you for listening yesterday. It really made me feel better."

"I'm glad I could help."

"Yeah," he said with a grin. "You helped my brain shift from total depression to mania in like, twenty minutes. I think that's a new record for me."

"And then you couldn't sleep," I said with a wince. "Sorry about that."

He waved me off and took a sip of coffee. "I'm

used to not sleeping. I never got a lot of it at my house."

I tried to imagine my own comfortable bed at home, with all its colorful pillows, but then I remembered the fire. Those pillows—and everything else in my room—were nothing but piles of ash now.

"I can't sleep here." I picked up my coffee cup as emphasis. "I'm too afraid of having a bad dream."

He grimaced. "I can relate. My dreams usually rehash every bad thing I've ever done. It's torture."

"Yeah, that's hard too. It's usually just hard to tell if mine are real or not." I glanced up at him quickly. "That probably sounds crazy."

He held out a hand to indicate the surrounding room. "We *are* in a mental facility. When in Rome, right?"

I relaxed and took a sip of coffee. The bitter taste made me wince. "So what's your story? What brought you here?"

"Wow, how much time do you have?" When I scoffed, he grinned back at me. It faded as he continued. "I had a hard childhood with just my mom. She did her best, but I was pretty out of control, even as a little kid. That was before the bipolar diagnosis. It made me do some risky things with a bunch of kids who were already legit criminals. My diagnosis kept me out of jail, I guess, but now I'm here."

"Were you in a gang?" I asked, though I found his whole story hard to believe. Aaron was the last person here I would peg to hang out with a bunch of criminals.

"You could say that," he said with a shrug. "We didn't have much money, and that makes people desperate."

I nodded even though I couldn't relate. "Jail for what?"

"People got hurt because of me," he said, and his face closed off in such a way that I knew he wouldn't elaborate.

"I know how that feels," I said, thinking of the dreams and premonitions I had before my sister and Katelyn died. And maybe it wasn't real, but I couldn't help the way I felt. "Sometimes I can't sleep because I feel so guilty."

He paused taking a sip of coffee. "That's what Lisa said, too. We had a lot in common."

I know he didn't mean it to make me feel bad, but sharp needles of jealousy pricked under my skin anyway. Lisa was relatable, but I wasn't?

Ugh, I groaned inwardly, *why are you even focused on*

something like that? You're in a mental facility. You should focus on getting out of here.

We both went quiet for a while after that. He ate the rest of his breakfast, and I choked down my coffee. I told myself I didn't want or need a boyfriend right now, and maybe Becca had a point about needing to focus on getting better. If he really had just been with Lisa before she left, I couldn't deny the possibility that he was just looking for a rebound.

But then I thought about what Danny said—that a relationship here could be helpful. Would it really be so wrong, then? I stole a glance at Aaron's handsome profile, and my heart skipped a little in my chest. He intrigued me, and he got me out of my head for five seconds. It was a lot more fun to think about Aaron than my delusions and anxieties.

"So, will your parents be coming this afternoon?" Aaron asked after he finished his plate of food and pushed it aside.

My hand shook a little while adding cream and sugar to my second cup of coffee. I shot him a confused look. "Why would they?"

"Parents are allowed to visit every two weeks here. Didn't anyone tell you?"

"No," I said as my whole body tried to process

this news. I wasn't sure I even wanted to see them after they'd abandoned me here. Especially now that I wondered if I'd been having delusions all along. I didn't want to see their smug faces when I had to admit they were right.

I knew they'd come, though. They were the type who would, or at least my mom was. She never missed an extracurricular activity—not that I had many. I was abysmal at sports, but I participated in art shows regularly. And of course, they went to every activity Amber had been involved in: cheer, dance, swimming.

"You look disgusted by this news—sorry about that," Aaron said.

"I just wasn't expecting it," I said, my stomach struggling to churn the bitter coffee now that it was knotted with anxiety. "I don't know what I want to say to them since they're the ones who dropped me off here."

"Well, hopefully they did the right thing for you, but I get why you'd feel mad about it. My mom won't even show up," Aaron said, tapping his fork on his tray with a down-turned expression. "She hasn't since the very first visit."

"That's horrible. I'm sorry." Not having them

visit at all would be worse. Then I really would feel abandoned.

He shrugged like it was no big deal, but I could see in his eyes that it was. He stood up and grabbed his tray. "Want me to throw your cup away for you?"

"I have a little left, but thanks."

"I'll see you later in group, okay?"

I nodded and watched him walk away. The fact that he had told me about his past warmed my heart, like we had really connected beyond stolen looks during group.

But then I thought about what he'd said about parents visiting. For some reason, I couldn't imagine seeing them here. Only a week ago, I would have looked forward to the chance to tear into them for abandoning me here. Now, though, after deciding I probably had some serious issues I needed to work on, I was pretty sure this was the right place to be after all. I still didn't know what exactly I would say to them. That I realized I had a problem? That I forgave them for bringing me here?

I didn't know if I was ready for that.

I wasn't sure I ever would be.

Because whenever I thought about my parents, this huge wave of hatred rose within me, like a tsunami threatening just offshore. It was the type of feeling that had the potential to drown me. Something about my past tried to bob to the surface of my mind, but I couldn't face it.

Not yet.

It was a good thing no one had told me about the parent visitation day thing until just a few hours ago because by the time it rolled around, I transformed into a shaky mess. The three cups of coffee were partially to blame. I'd been to the bathroom five times thanks to all the caffeine and anxiety pumping through my system.

All twenty-four of us waited for them in the rec room because it had the most space. The windows revealed a storm gray sky outside, and the cold seeped through the thin glass.

Becca and I sat together at one of the tables, waiting for our parents. She looked as laid-back as ever, but Becca also hid her emotions well. I kept squirming in my seat to distract myself from my racing heart and tight chest.

"Have your parents come every time?" I asked her.

"Just my mom. Sometimes with my older sister. I

like when my sister comes because she tells me stuff I actually want to hear. The latest TikTok trends and what's up with my friends online. My mom just demands that I hurry up and get better."

Amber would never have done that for me. We weren't close like that. She tended to think that anything I liked was lame. But it still sent a shard of pain through my heart to hear about someone else's sister coming to visit. Mine never would again.

"Yeah, I wish they'd let us have our phones in here," I said.

Becca shook her head. "I don't. I get way too hung up on what everyone is saying about me online. And then I never sleep. I just obsessively check it."

"I guess that's true," I said, even though I couldn't remember a lot of my day-to-day activities before I came here. When I tried to think back before my parents dropped me off, I just remembered the fire. My sister's screams.

I slammed a door shut on that line of thinking and tried to focus on something else instead. I noticed Aaron sitting on the couch reading. He wasn't watching the entrance of the rec room like everyone else.

"I feel so bad for Aaron that his parents never visit," I said.

Becca gave me a strange look and opened her mouth to say something, but then the nurses arrived, leading a line of parents and family members.

"Aw, just my mom came," Becca said with a sigh. "I'll see you later, Sadie."

My parents didn't come with the first group, but it was early yet. Both of Danny's parents came and enveloped him in huge hugs that brought a smile to my face. Jon's dad came and listened to him talk with sympathetic eyes. Millie's mom, and what looked like her grandparents came. Her grandmother held her hand and talked nonstop—probably to make up for Millie's silence.

I kept stealing glances at Aaron, but he never looked up from his book.

Every time a family member walked into the room, my heart leapt into my throat. After a while, though, they stopped coming in at all.

Face burning, I walked over to the aide, Pete, beside the door. He watched me with the usual suspicion all the aides gave us when we approached them. Like they all expected us to ask if they would help us escape or something. "Hey, do you know if my parents are just running late?"

Pete's expression slowly shifted to a sympathetic

look. "I'm sorry, but this is everybody who's coming. They had to call ahead to let us know."

Until Pete said that, I really thought they might just be running late.

Something dark and ugly rose so fast inside me it made my head swim. How could they just leave me here? I thought of my increasing panic attacks and trauma over the loss of my sister. So they just didn't want to deal with it? They didn't want to deal with *me*?

To Pete, I just nodded and walked away because I didn't trust my voice. Telling myself that no one was watching my humiliation because they were too busy with their families, I kept my head down as I crossed the room, standing awkwardly beside the table where I'd been sitting, unsure of what to do.

"Sadie," Aaron called from the couch. He patted the seat beside him. "Come sit here."

A rush of gratitude washed over me as I made my way to the couch and sat down heavily.

"I'm sorry they didn't show," he said quietly.

"They're probably just really busy," I said, but I was fooling no one, least of all myself.

Tears slipped down my cheeks as Aaron put his arm around my shoulders.

Maybe they had finally just given up on me.

15

I had never been close to my parents. They weren't exactly the type of people you shared all your thoughts and dreams with. My mom listened to my sister, but she didn't listen to me. I hardly even saw my dad because he traveled so much for work. We didn't have family dinners, and I doubted they even knew what classes I had enrolled in, much less my interests outside of art. My mom never missed taking me to a therapy appointment, but only because she didn't want to risk renewing my prescription for meds.

Given all these things I knew about my parents, expecting they would come to visit me in a mental facility seemed like an especially stupid assumption. I hated myself a little for getting my hopes up for two people who had rarely been there for me.

But no matter what I told myself, it still hurt. I cried myself to sleep that first night. When I woke up the next morning, I had Millie's stuffed dog tucked under my arm. I hugged it with a slight smile tugging at my lips and put it back on Millie's neatly made bed.

A few days later, the threatening gray skies had brought the rarest of weather to Georgia: snow. This happened maybe every few years if we were lucky. The snow never stuck around long—only a day or two most of the time. Usually only a light dusting coated everything, but to us, we felt like we'd suddenly been transported to Alaska.

We all gathered in Julia's group room, faces pressed to the window. An inch or two of snow covered the world outside, beckoning us to come play.

If we were all home, we would get a snow day from school. Everything would be shut down: schools, buses, businesses. A snow day meant a brief vacation from all our responsibilities. Since we were in a mental facility, though, we didn't know if we would get to enjoy it the same way.

So, as soon as Julia walked into the group room, we begged her for a break.

"All we can think about is the snow," Becca said. "You gotta let us go out there."

"Yeah, we can do our feelings check-in while we build a snowman," Danny added.

Jon's arms were crossed over his chest. "That doesn't seem like enough snow for a snowman."

"Shut up," someone hissed at him.

Julia laughed. "All right, all right. I was already planning to take y'all out there. But listen, it's cold. You're going to need coats and gloves—whatever you came here in. So Pete here," she nodded at where he stood leaning against the wall, "will take you to the storage room to get them."

We all cheered, just happy to be able to go out in the snow. When we all first got here, we had to leave our personal belongings behind in a locked room. You know, kinda like jail. I had a puffer jacket and no gloves, so I knew I would freeze, but it would still be worth it.

Pete led us to the room and unlocked the door. Our stuff was packed away in clear plastic bags labeled "belongings" that felt very clinical.

"I'm going to call each of you one at a time,

okay?" Pete said, eyeballing us like we really were in prison.

"Damn, there goes my plan to steal my phone," Jon said loudly. Pete's eyes narrowed. Clearly that was what he expected us to do.

After we spent half of group sorting through our stuff and trying to find enough warm clothes that would work, we finally made it outside. For just a moment, we all stood still. There was something about a fresh snowfall that seemed so pristine. It softened the unruly bushes that badly needed trimming. It covered the patchy brown grass and hid the shriveled flower beds. The skeletal trees glittered in the sunlight, looking whimsical instead of nightmarish.

Danny made a sound that was very close to a squeal of delight, and then the quiet spell was broken. We dashed out into the sparkling snow, grabbing handfuls wherever the piles were thick enough.

Jon scooped up a big clump of snow and quickly formed it into a ball. He chucked it at Aaron, who immediately returned fire.

And then suddenly we were all in on it— choosing sides right away. Millie joined Jon's team while I sided with Aaron. Becca and Danny were both on Jon's team, too. Other kids from group who I didn't know as well joined Aaron's team. Very soon it became Aaron and me against our friends. We grinned stupidly at each other, and I couldn't help feeling drawn to him—no matter what Becca said.

We dashed behind trees and benches, trying to form snowballs quickly and pelt each other. Unfortunately, none of us had much experience making them, so they mostly fell apart in the air. I managed to hit Becca in the chest, and the loosely packed snowball exploded on impact, spraying her with snow.

The boys were yelling random military-ish phrases like, "Fire at will!" and "Duck and cover!" It couldn't be cheesier, but everyone screamed and laughed as we raced to find cover and return fire.

At one point, Millie and I were squared off against each other. I couldn't stop laughing because every ball I formed disintegrated in my cold hands. Millie was having similar trouble, so we both kept throwing useless sprays of snowflakes.

Finally, I managed to form a hard-packed snowball that would keep its shape. I lifted my arm to throw it at her, and she held her hands up.

"No!" she yelled with a laugh.

The snowball and my mouth dropped at the same time.

Millie's eyes widened.

"Did you just . . . ?" I asked as Aaron and Becca came over to us.

"What happened?" Becca asked, cheeks flushed from the cold.

"Millie just yelled 'no' at me," I said, still smiling at the surprised wonder on her face.

Becca threw her arms around Millie and hugged her tight. "That's amazing!"

"That's awesome, Millie," Aaron said with a smile.

Danny, Jon, and the others came to see what we were all excited about, and when news spread that Millie had said her first word since she'd been here, everyone was quick to congratulate her. I thought about what Becca had said when I first met Millie: that she hadn't spoken anything in years. Now, she had not only said something, but she was beaming and standing taller than I'd ever seen her do.

My heart swelled.

Julia must have noticed how we were all surrounding Millie because she came over to us. "What's going on?"

"Millie said 'no' when I was about to hit her with a snowball," I told her.

"Millie! I am so proud of you," she said, smiling widely. She put her arm around Millie's thin shoulders and gave her a little squeeze. "This is cause for celebration. How about some hot chocolate?"

While everyone cheered, I had a flash of a memory: Amber and I drinking hot chocolate together on Christmas Eve. Our mother had fixed the cups and let us add whipped cream.

It seemed like I never had just purely happy memories like this one. Usually I also remembered something bad at the same time, like that later Amber and I fought. But not this time. I only remembered the warmth inside my chest as we drank hot chocolate with Mom. After that, we'd watched a Christmas movie together.

I felt like that now. Calm and happy.

I couldn't remember the last time I hadn't felt anxiety or had obsessive thoughts. It had been a long time since I'd felt anything close to happiness. But right now, even with freezing cold hands, there was a lightness in my chest, like a snowflake falling gently.

I never wanted this feeling to end.

We gathered in the kitchen, and even the cold, industrial metal counters couldn't deflate my mood. Julia got out a huge tin of powdered hot chocolate mix, and then she heated up a big pot of water on the stove. This definitely wouldn't be gourmet drinking chocolate or anything, but it was sweet and would warm us up quick.

"My grandmother used to make me hot chocolate any time I visited and it was remotely cold outside," Julia said with a smile as she handed out steaming Dixie cups. "It's how she showed her love."

Not all of us had the kind and caring grandmother who lived to spoil us, but at least today, we could pretend someone cared enough to fix us a treat.

We passed the cups around, and then she got out big cans of whipped cream to spray on top. Julia walked around to everyone's cup offering the cream.

Millie held hers out with a smile, and when she got some, she said in a quiet voice, "Thank you."

Julia nearly dropped the can. "Did you really just say that?" she whispered.

Millie nodded, her eyes shiny with emotion.

"It's so good to hear your voice, Millie," Julia

said, and her own cracked like she was holding back tears.

It was the first time I realized the counselors might truly care about us. At least Julia did. I still had my doubts about Dr. Williams, though. He just seemed dead inside.

Seeing Millie not only saying something for the first time in years but also smiling happily brought a burst of hope to my own heart. If someone who had struggled that much—the selective mutism, the slinking around like a stray dog that had been kicked too many times—could get better, maybe there was hope for the rest of us. Even if I was dealing with delusions and obsessive thoughts, it couldn't be as bad as overcoming total silence. Would Millie now start to talk about whatever had made her go quiet in the first place? A little shudder ran down my spine. It must have been something massively traumatic.

Like a family member abusing her, I thought out of nowhere. Suddenly disgusted, I put my cup of half-finished hot chocolate down on the counter. Why did I sometimes have messed-up thoughts like that? Where did they come from?

"We're going to need more hot chocolate and whipped cream to celebrate," Julia said as she started refilling everyone's cups.

I couldn't drink anymore, though.

Before Julia could refill Millie's cup, Dr. Williams walked into the kitchen, his bushy brows furrowed. Without really knowing why, I hunched my shoulders and tried not to look at him. "What's going on in here?"

"We're celebrating," Julia said with a conspiratorial smile toward all of us.

"I hope it's for something good and not just because it's snowing outside," he said.

I gritted my teeth because that was such an asshole thing to say. Why were some people like that? They had to make jerkish comments no matter the situation. It was like they couldn't stand when everyone else was happy.

"Millie spoke today," Julia said, still smiling hard like her baby had said her first words.

"Incredible, Millie," Dr. Williams said, his eyes wide. "What brought this on?"

"Well she said, 'thank you' to me, but that was actually the second thing she said." Her gaze landed on me. "Sadie, do you want to tell Dr. Williams what happened?"

I cleared my throat as everyone stared at me. Dr. Williams's head swung my way like he was particularly interested. "We were having a snowball fight, and I finally managed to make a good ball to throw at Millie—all the others had just fallen apart. We were both laughing at that, but then when I went to throw the snowball at her, she yelled, 'No!' But like, in a joking way."

"This is truly amazing," he said. "A real breakthrough. Millie," he turned to her and held out his hand, "would you mind coming with me? I think now would be a good time to have a therapy session and see if we can capitalize on your mind's willingness to allow speech again."

Millie nodded shyly and put down her hot chocolate.

"Bring it with you," Julia said, handing it back to her freshly refilled.

Millie took it with another sweet smile and followed Dr. Williams out of the kitchen.

Everyone else resumed drinking hot chocolate and talking, but I couldn't bring myself to join in. I didn't like how Dr. Williams seemed annoyed by our celebration. He didn't even act that happy for Millie. And why was he immediately hauling her away? Like she wanted to sit down and endure more therapy right now. If he had treated me like that, I wouldn't want to open my mouth again. But that was a psychiatrist for you. They had to question things to death.

Hopefully, he would suppress his natural psychiatrist urges and praise her for speaking after all these years. It was the least he could do.

That night, Millie came back to our room after having spent hours away with Dr. Williams. She never even came to dinner. What had he been doing? Interrogating her? When I heard her come into the room, slinking by with her shoulders hunched, I sat up in bed.

"Millie?"

She hurried into bed without even glancing my way, but I could tell her eyes looked haunted.

"Are you okay?" I tried again.

But she made no attempt to respond to me. She covered herself with a blanket even though our room felt warm. Eventually, I lay back down and tried to read my book with the weak light from under the door.

She never spoke another word.

16

I blamed the dream on having fun in the snow today. All that time spent outdoors made me let down my guard and fall asleep easily for once.

The dream had a nightmarish quality from the start. I stumbled down the hallway of the mental facility, dark shadows crouched like gargoyles around every turn. Fear gripped me so hard I could barely breathe. My bladder ached. I needed to pee, but the thought of going into the bathroom had my heart seizing in my chest. Something horrible waited there. Something much worse than shadowy gargoyles.

The air around me thrummed with tension. The walls had eyes, watching as I struggled to take each step. My bladder urged me on, even as my mind said on repeat, *Don't go in there.*

I tried to stop, but my feet carried me forward almost against my will. I reached out and grabbed hold of the doorknob. My hand looked grotesquely pale in the eerie light.

The door creaked as I pushed it open.

The smell hit me first, even before the automatic lights flickered to life. It knocked me back, my lip curling in disgust. That was an instinctual reaction, but it took my mind a few moments to register what I smelled.

It was the coppery scent of blood. So much of it that it felt like it coated the insides of my nostrils.

The bright fluorescent lights revealed the scene before me, and I opened my mouth to scream. No sound escaped, even as I gazed down at Millie's broken body.

***

I awoke with a painful gasp, my heart clawing at my throat. A dream. Just a dream. For a moment, I lay there, breathing hard. I put my hand on my stomach like Julia showed us. While I tried to force my breaths to slow down, my heart continued to thud loudly in my ears.

Something wet ran down my cheek, and I realized I had tears in my eyes.

Millie, I thought.

This was why I was afraid to go to sleep at night. I should have gone to Dr. Williams and asked for something to help with the nightmares. The intensity of this dream seemed off the chart. I could still smell the blood, and I had never woken up crying from a dream before.

The room was still dark. I looked over at Millie's side of the room, but the pile of blankets made it difficult to see. I crept over to her bed, tripping over her stuffed dog in the process.

"Millie?" I whispered, not wanting to freak her out if she wasn't awake yet.

I reached down and touched the pile of blankets. My hand stilled.

Her bed was empty.

This is just a hallucination, I told myself even as a cold fear gripped me. Maybe none of this was real. Maybe I still lay in my bed, dreaming.

I ran my hand over my arm and gently slapped the skin. A tiny sting. I did it a little harder, and the pain lasted longer.

Not a dream then.

Millie's probably just brushing her teeth, I thought while another, quieter voice whispered, *She always makes her bed first.*

I hurried out of our room.

I ran to the bathroom, arriving much faster than I did in my dream. No one was around yet. I hadn't checked the time, but I thought it was probably early—before the new shift of nurses and techs arrived.

I pushed open the door. Just like my dream, the smell hit me first. Thick and coppery. I whimpered.

The lights flickered on.

Millie lay on the floor, arms outstretched. Angry slashes tore her wrists, and a piece of jagged glass lay beside her. Blood pooled around her body. It had even seeped into her hair, turning the ends red.

Her face was twisted in a grimace, and her eyes were wide and unseeing.

I opened my mouth to scream.

This time, I screamed and screamed and didn't stop until there were footsteps behind me.

Was I trapped in a nightmare? How did I know any of this was real?

Jax arrived first. He practically dragged me out of the bathroom, and I fought him every step of the way. I had no control over my reactions. It felt like I floated above my body, looking down on it. I could still feel the horror of the situation, but it was muffled. Insulated. So many people rushed in: other kids, mental health techs, nurses. Through the open bathroom door, I saw a flurry of activity around Millie, but I knew it was too late.

"Get these kids out of here!" one of the nurses shouted.

Becca came out of the bathroom, pushed from behind by a tech. She sobbed like her heart had been ripped from her chest. The sound echoed in my ears, threatening to tear me apart.

I didn't suffer from any sensory disorders, but at that moment, it seemed like I did. I covered my ears to try and drown out the cacophony of sounds. The nurses barking orders, the screams of horror from each new person who saw Millie, the sobs of all the girls who had known her.

Jax placed his big hand on my arm, the warmth

seeping through my scrubs. "Are you the one who found her?"

I nodded slowly.

"Okay, I think we need to get you to Dr. Williams."

I would have rather seen Julia, but I couldn't say that. My throat had closed up. Everything had a surreal quality to it, like we were all trapped inside a horror movie.

Please let none of this be real. Please let me be dreaming.

I couldn't cry or move or speak. It was like Millie's spirit had passed on her selective mutism.

Jax put his hands on my shoulders and gently steered me away. I followed docilely, like some kind of dumbfounded sheep.

When we got to Dr. Williams's office, a dam broke inside me. The truth clawed itself to the tip of my tongue, desperate to be free. I had dreamed about her death before it manifested into reality. I really was psychic—it wasn't a delusion.

"She was the first to find Millie," Jax told Dr. Williams in low tones.

Dr. Williams ushered me in and showed me to his ugly couch. I didn't sit. I stood, shaking and wild-eyed.

Dr. Williams and Jax shared a look.

"Sadie," Dr. Williams said carefully, "Jax told me you were the first to find poor Millie. That must have been a terrible shock."

My head shot up, and I looked him in the eyes. "It wasn't a shock at all—I knew I would find her like that. It was just like my dream."

He leaned away from me. "You saw Millie die in a dream?"

"I'm saying I saw her dead with slashed wrists. It was so intense I could smell her blood. And then when I woke up, she wasn't in our room. I went straight to the bathroom because that's where I found her in my nightmare."

Dr. Williams cleared his throat. "Sadie, this will be hard to hear right now because you're so understandably upset, but thinking you dreamed her death is another delusion. Just like what you experienced after your sister's death. You couldn't have known. No one could have."

I shook my head emphatically. "No, I dreamed that. I'm sure of it. How else would I have known to look for her there?"

"It's a natural place to find her first thing in the morning," Dr. Williams said in a frustratingly calm tone.

"You always have an explanation for everything,

don't you?" I practically spat at him. "Then why did you spend so much time with her yesterday?" I asked, pacing closer to him. "What did you say to her? Maybe *you're* the reason she's dead!" I jabbed a finger right at his chest.

His face had lost that bored expression. I could see the whites of his eyes as he made a hurried gesture at Jax, who came over immediately and took hold of my arms.

"Let's just sit down and relax, Sadie," Jax said.

But the second he tried to steer me toward the couch, panic exploded inside me like a grenade. All I could think was that if I wasn't delusional, then what did it mean? Millie couldn't have killed herself.

"What did you do to her?" I demanded.

I tried to jerk my arm out of Jax's grasp. He tightened his hold. It set something off within me, something primal. I tried to free myself in earnest now, tugging and rolling and fighting. Jax had to use his considerable weight advantage to hold me down.

Dr. Williams went over to a supply cabinet behind his desk and opened it. When he retrieved a syringe, I screamed and thrashed.

"No! Don't drug me! Don't silence me!"

Jax's face was one big grimace. "I'm sorry about this, Sadie."

Dr. Williams offered no such apology.

A huge sting on my upper thigh made my body tense up like a bow. Warmth spread as the drug moved through my bloodstream. My muscles weakened, and I could no longer fight back. My vision blurred and darkened as my breathing slowed.

They continued to hold me down.

What if I suffocate to death? I thought.

But then I couldn't think anything else at all.

17

I awoke with a scream trapped in my throat. I opened my eyes blearily as memories trickled back into my conscious mind. Each one made my breaths come faster.

Fighting wildly while Jax restrained me and Dr. Williams injected me with a sedative.

Dreaming that I found Millie dead in the bathroom.

Finding Millie with her wrists slashed.

My mind flipped through images of Millie lying dead on the floor like the pages of a comic book. A pounding headache beat a painful rhythm behind my eyes, and I pressed both hands to the sides of my head.

Had it all been a nightmare? With my mind

foggy from whatever drug I'd been given, reality seemed a slippery thing to catch hold of.

Swallowing hard, I glanced over at Millie's bed. The blankets looked the same, tangled and balled up on the mattress. Her threadbare stuffed puppy still lay in the same place on the floor.

A sob bubbled up out of nowhere, and I cried for the loss of the girl who was just beginning to find her voice again. I thought of the way she kept her shoulders hunched protectively around her ears when I first got here, and how I later got to see her smile and even laugh.

How could she be dead? How could she have killed herself?

I thought of her mom and her grandparents. What would they say when they heard what happened? Would they be confused after just seeing her a few days ago, alive and well? The way she'd laughingly told me "no" flitted through my head. Did Julia and Dr. Williams let them know she'd made progress?

And now she was gone.

It didn't seem possible.

Suddenly, I couldn't stand to be in my room another second.

With my hand on my pounding forehead, I

pulled open my door. I nearly ran into Jax waiting just outside.

"Whoa, it's okay," he said, holding up his hands as I backed away like a skittish horse.

I watched him for any threat of a needle. "What are you doing here?"

"I'm here to make sure you're feeling better," he said.

Translation: *I'm here to restrain you if you lose your shit again.*

"What time is it? Don't you work night shift?"

He consulted his watch. "It's five-thirty. You've been asleep about twelve hours. And yes, I typically work nights, but Dr. Williams had me go home to sleep and then come right back."

Dr. Williams obviously thought he would need his help with me again.

I glared at him accusingly.

He held his hands up. "I get that you're mad at me, but we couldn't let you be that agitated. You were becoming a danger to yourself and others."

"Now you're going to follow me all around to see if I'm fixing to lose it?"

He just raised his bushy brows. "Are you?"

"I'm going to take a shower right now. That's what I'm going to do."

I marched past him, knowing he'd have to call a female tech if he wanted to continue to make sure I didn't lose my mind. He didn't move to follow me, so I breathed out a sigh of relief. When I got to the bathroom, I refused to look at the place where I found Millie. From the corner of my eye, I saw that the tiles were white again, but I scurried past it so fast I couldn't make out much detail.

Basic shower supplies were kept in a storage closet inside the bathroom, and I helped myself to cheap soap, shampoo, and conditioner. We didn't even get razors to shave with. I grabbed a scratchy towel and headed toward a shower stall.

As the hot water hit my body, my mind cycled through the events of the past few weeks. After I had been wrong about Jon's imminent death, I had convinced myself that I was delusional and not psychic at all. But what if it was possible to change someone's fate? Maybe he really had been contemplating suicide, and my psychic—what, power? Ability?—picked up on it. But then later he decided not to go through with it. Maybe all my obsessive questions had gotten through to him.

With Katelyn and Amber, I had that horrible feeling that preceded the dreams of their deaths. But with Millie, I only had that terrible nightmare but not the feeling. Why?

I puzzled over it as I lathered a rag masquerading as a washcloth with soap.

What if Millie's decision to end her life was a last minute one? Maybe that was why I didn't get a warning in the form of a psychic feeling.

I thought of the way Millie had spoken her first word to me in the snow, pain cutting through me at the thought of her soft smile and bright eyes. And, later, when we had hot chocolate with her, she had spoken again, and the pride reflected in her eyes had been unmistakable. What had happened from that moment to when she wanted to kill herself?

I froze as I watched the soap suds go down the drain. Millie had spent hours in Dr. Williams's office right after our celebration, and she had returned to the room clearly upset. What had they talked about? What upset her so much she later decided to kill herself?

The next thought hit me so hard I gasped and accidentally swallowed shower water. I coughed and sputtered, my mind working overtime. Katelyn spent hours in Dr. Williams's office before her suicide, too.

What did that mean?

What were the chances of two suicides at the

same mental health facility within a week of each other? Especially when both victims never acted suicidal beforehand.

No, something was definitely up. There were too many coincidences.

But what if it's just my crazy mind telling me these things? I wondered.

I didn't know how to answer that. How could you tell if your own thoughts were delusional?

But then I remembered I wasn't alone. Becca cared about what had happened to Millie. Danny cared about Katelyn. We all cared about kids we had talked and laughed with suddenly dying in violent ways, whether it was suicide or not.

The other kids could help me figure out what was going on. I couldn't just let this go. Not this time.

I didn't see Becca until after dinner because neither of us could stomach a meal. I made do with a pack of graham crackers and the small tubs of peanut butter they gave us whenever we were desperate for a snack. I ate it alone in my room, but I couldn't look at Millie's bed. Especially since someone had come and stripped her blankets. They took the stuffed puppy, too. The graham crackers and peanut butter got stuck in my throat at the thought that I'd never see her again. It didn't seem real. After eating as much of the snack as I could, I went looking for Becca.

She stood in the empty group room, staring out the window into the garden beyond. Now that the snow had all but disappeared, the view was hideous again. Naked, twisting trees, untrimmed bushes, dead grass, blackened flowers. The wonderland that we'd had a snowball fight in just yesterday seemed like a dream now.

I sat down beside Becca, and she glanced over at me. Her characteristic dark eye makeup was missing, and her eyes were bloodshot from crying.

"I just didn't see this coming, you know?" she said, her voice thick. "We all said that about Katelyn, but I mean, Millie . . ." She let out a pained sob.

Her distress triggered tears stinging my own eyes. "It doesn't make sense, does it? Millie had just made the first major progress in years. She seemed so happy."

Becca nodded emphatically. "That's what I kept telling myself, too. Like, how could Millie go from smiling and happy and—talking!—to killing herself later that night?"

At least that much hadn't been faulty memory or a product of my delusional mind. Becca had seen Millie acting happy after speaking her first words, too.

"Have there ever been suicides here? This close together?"

She wiped her nose on her sleeve and turned to look at me. "I overheard the nurses talking about it. They said the last suicide here was almost ten years ago. And now there have been two. In a row."

I took that in. "There really is something going on here," I said, more to myself than to Becca.

"If nothing else, it's suspicious as hell."

"Did you know both Katelyn and Millie went to see Dr. Williams and came out upset right before they died?"

She searched my face. "What are you saying?"

"I don't know. It's just weird, right? There are a lot of similarities between the two even though they died in different ways. Like, both were completely unexpected with no signs they felt suicidal. Both happened shortly after going to see Dr. Williams and getting upset—"

"Both happened around the same time," Becca interrupted.

"I didn't even realize that before, but you're

right." Of course I was thinking about the other similarity between the two deaths—the fact that I had dreamed about them first. I couldn't tell Becca that, though. Not if I wanted her to take me seriously and help figure out what was going on.

"What do we do?" I asked. "We obviously can't go to Dr. Williams about all this."

She shook her head. "No." After a moment of thinking she said, "We need to have a meeting after lights out. Danny, Aaron, Jon, and us."

"That's a good idea. Where should we meet?"

"The kitchen is the best place because they never go in there after we've all gone to bed."

We both agreed to spread the word and meet as soon as we could slip past the mental health techs.

I walked back to my room, my chest already feeling lighter. Together we would find out what was going on.

I just wouldn't tell them about my part in it: that I had dreamed their deaths before they even happened.

Later that night, the five of us met by the soft glow of the light above the big stove in the kitchen. We all wore matching grief-stricken faces, but something else hid beneath the shadows and bags under our eyes.

An undercurrent of fear.

Danny and Jon stood close enough that their arms touched, but Aaron stood apart from them, his expression guarded. Becca and I faced the boys on one side of the kitchen island.

"This isn't just another memorial in Millie's honor," Becca said. "Sadie wanted us to meet and talk about the suspicious shit going on around here lately."

The three boys turned expectant gazes on me.

I cleared my throat and tried to ignore the butterflies in my stomach at the sudden attention. "I told Becca earlier that the ways Katelyn and Millie died have some suspicious similarities. Like the fact that neither of them seemed suicidal in the least." I looked specifically at Danny when I said this.

Danny nodded. "I always said I had no idea Katelyn was suicidal. I'm still not convinced she was, except that she's no longer with us."

"Same with Millie—she'd just spoken her first

words in years," I said, "so why would she want to suddenly kill herself?"

"Tell them what you told me about Dr. Williams," Becca said.

This got raised eyebrows from Danny and Jon. Aaron just quietly waited.

"Both Millie and Katelyn went to see Dr. Williams before they died and came out of those meetings looking traumatized. Millie was in there with him for hours. When she got back to our room, she looked honestly disturbed. It gets weirder, though. I saw Katelyn come out of Dr. Williams's office before she died, and she was sobbing."

"I knew something was up with that shrink," Becca said with a curl to her lip.

Aaron spoke up for the first time. "That's pretty messed up to keep Millie in there for hours, too."

Jon nodded. "I remembered thinking it was weird that he wanted to talk to her in the middle of us celebrating. Like, couldn't it wait, jackass?"

I took a deep breath before continuing because I knew the next thing I was about to say was more than a little out there. "I also think maybe Millie and Katelyn saw something they shouldn't have. Like, maybe someone wanted to keep them quiet and just make it *look* like they committed suicide."

I watched them with my shoulders tensed, waiting for them to declare me completely insane.

"I can almost guarantee Katelyn didn't kill herself," Danny said with conviction.

"Millie wouldn't either," Becca said.

I let out my breath. "Then what really happened to them?"

"Dr. Williams has always been sus," Becca said. "I say we get into his office and see what we can find."

We all looked at her in surprise, but then Jon scoffed. "What do you think is in there, some long note about how he caused them to kill themselves or something?"

Becca narrowed her eyes at his smartass comment. "I mean, that isn't the craziest thought in the world considering he has case files on all of us in there."

"Just the idea of sneaking in his office gives me hives," Danny said, scratching his arm.

"I'll go," I said. "This was my idea to investigate, so I'll take the risks."

"Man, if you get caught, though . . ." Aaron said with a worried frown.

"He usually leaves pretty early," Becca said. "I

think she'll be fine. And I know where I can swipe his keys."

"Where?" I asked.

"They keep an extra set in the nurse's station, and night shift leaves it wide open all the time when they wander off to go to the bathroom or go outside to smoke or whatever."

"You are super resourceful, Bex," Danny said, coming around his side of the island to put his arm around her and give her a little squeeze. "I wouldn't want to get on your bad side."

"What can we do to make sure Sadie doesn't get caught?" Aaron asked, his jaw still tight with what seemed like concern. Warmth bloomed inside me at the thought. It was nice to feel like someone wanted to watch out for me.

"We need to make sure all the techs are occupied," Becca said.

"I can handle that," Jon said, rubbing his hands together.

Becca and I shared a look. "You just seem way too eager," Becca said. "Do I even want to know?"

"I'm thinking it's going to involve a lot of shit," Jon said with a grin.

Danny groaned. "I really hope you don't mean that literally."

Jon just waggled his eyebrows.

"Okay, well, I'll be in charge of distracting whoever is on the girl's side," Becca said.

"So, when's this going down?" Jon asked, an eager gleam in his eyes. "Tonight?"

"No," I said with a shake of my head.

"You don't even have a diversion yet, and the night is halfway over," Becca snapped at him with an eye roll.

"We'll need a little more time," I said. "Tomorrow night is better."

We went over a few more details, but it felt like a huge weight had been lifted from my shoulders.

Like I would finally get to the bottom of what was happening here.

And whether I was actually psychic . . .

Or seriously insane.

18

After our meeting in the kitchen, Aaron pulled me aside while the others continued back to their rooms. In the dim light of the kitchen, his face looked tight with concern.

"I'm really worried about this plan," he said.

Two emotions warred inside me. One was a sharp bite of annoyance because I didn't want anyone to dissuade me from finally finding out the truth. The other was a spreading warmth in my chest that he cared that much. I tried to focus on the more pleasant emotion. "Why?"

"I don't want you to get caught. Trust me, I know a thing or two about sneaking around and doing stuff you're not supposed to. Even here, you'll be in huge trouble."

I scoffed. "They'll probably just say I'm a danger to myself and others again and inject me with whatever that is that makes me sleep for a day. I've already survived it. Twice."

"I think it's more like they'll send you to isolation."

I waved him off. "That's only in prison."

"They have one here, too. It's a padded room."

That raised the hairs on the back of my neck. But I still couldn't let it stop me.

"We've met here twice and never been caught, so what's the difference if I snoop around Dr. Williams's office?"

"It's not far from the nurse's station, for one thing," he said. When I just sort of shrugged, he sighed and swiped a hand over his face. "I care about you, Sadie."

He took a step toward me and cupped my cheek. I couldn't look away. My heart pounded in my chest as my gaze dropped to his lips.

Aaron made this frustrated groan like he was fighting with himself, and then suddenly his head lowered to mine. Our lips touched, tentative at first, but then much more hungrily. Butterflies exploded within me, while at the same time, it felt like we had done this many times before. My body fit perfectly against his as our tongues moved in a familiar dance.

With a shuddering breath, Aaron took a step away from me, leaving my arms suddenly cold and empty.

"I probably shouldn't have done that," he said, running his fingers through his dark hair. "I know we're all supposed to be focusing on ourselves and getting better."

"I'm not sorry," I said. "Since when is kissing not allowed?"

He smiled. "I mean, it makes me feel a hell of a lot better than therapy does."

"No kidding. Especially when all Dr. Williams docs is try to make me think my every thought is crazy. He had me believing I was completely delusional, but now I'm not so sure."

"What do you mean?"

I hesitated. Dr. Williams was the only person I had tried to tell about my psychic abilities, and that had not gone well.

Would Aaron reject me, too?

Suddenly I was tired of keeping it to myself. Wondering if it was all in my head. I craved the sound of someone agreeing that it wasn't all coincidental, that it really did mean something to dream their deaths before they happened.

"It started with my sister," I said quietly. "I had this horrible feeling the night before she died. Like I was coming down with the flu, but maybe also on the verge of a panic attack." I rubbed my arm as goosebumps spread.

Aaron listened, and his open expression made me continue.

"That same night I had this horrible nightmare that she would die in a fire." His expression turned sympathetic. He probably already knew where this was going. "And in the morning, I woke up, coughing in the grass in the front yard. Two fire trucks full of firemen were there trying to put out the flames, but my house was completely engulfed. My sister was inside."

"Shit, Sadie, I'm so sorry. That's traumatic."

"I still don't really remember how I made it out. The memories I have of that night are from the nightmare. It was so real I can still smell the smoke and hear my sister's screams."

He reached out and hugged me, and I let myself relax in his strong arms.

"That was traumatic enough," I said, pulling away so I could look at him again, "but then the same thing happened here. Before Katelyn died," I added when he raised his eyebrows.

"You had that same feeling?"

I nodded. "I had this bad feeling in group while she was talking, and then right after that, I had this horrible image in my mind of her dying. Then that night, I dreamed about it." Before he could say anything else, I rushed ahead. "And I know I really had that dream because it was different from how she died. In my nightmare, I dreamed someone stood over her and choked her."

"When in reality, they found her hanging," he said, thoughtfully.

"Yeah, and that was confusing. With Millie, I didn't get that feeling, but I still had the dream. This time, the dream was exactly what happened. I saw her lying on the bathroom floor with her wrists slashed, and when I woke up and ran there in the morning, that's exactly what I found."

"That had to have been terrifying," he said, but I couldn't tell from his tone if he believed me or not.

"The dreams were all so vivid and real. Now I wonder if they were trying to tell me something— that they didn't just die. They were murdered."

Aaron stood there silently while heat creeped up my neck. Did he think I'd gone too far?

"And that's why you want to get into his office so bad," he said slowly. "You want to see if your dreams really meant something."

"Exactly," I said with a huge rush of relief. He got it.

"I guess if I had potentially prophetic dreams like that, I would want to know what really happened, too."

I threw my arms around him and squeezed. "Thank you."

He chuckled. "What for?"

"Just listening to me. Especially when I'm basically saying I think there's a killer loose."

"I think we all have questions about two suicides in a row."

"It's messed up. There's just something about this place, too. I've felt it since the moment I got here. I still haven't figured out what happened to Lisa, for example." I said, momentarily forgetting that he had dated her. All I could think about was her name on my door sign and how no one told me whether she just left. "What if it's all some big conspiracy? What if someone killed her, too, and Dr. Williams covered it up?"

I hadn't even really been paying attention to

what I was saying. I was just thinking out loud. The effect it had on Aaron, though, happened instantly.

He took a step away from me, his face darkening.

"What?" I asked.

"What the hell, Sadie?" he demanded, his tone as harsh as his words. "I mean, I was willing to listen when you thought the suicides were suspicious and that you may have even dreamed about them first because hey, weird shit happens. But when you say something like this . . ." he trailed off, shaking his head. "You aren't well. You need serious help."

He stalked toward the door, and I reached out for him, but he jerked away. His eyes flashed as his hands curled into fists. Tension filled the air like a flash of lightning. For a terrible moment, I thought he would hit me.

"Just stay the fuck away from me," he snapped and kept walking.

Soon, I was alone in the kitchen, my stomach roiling like storm-tossed waves.

How did we go from kissing to him being so pissed off he acted like he might punch me? Why did everyone here get so shifty any time I mentioned Lisa?

But more importantly:

What really happened to Lisa?

I slept terribly. My anxiety turned into a living, breathing monster that sat on my chest and made it impossible for my lungs to expand. I couldn't even enjoy thoughts of kissing Aaron because the whole thing had been ruined by his reaction to what I said.

Every time I thought of him saying I needed serious help, I winced and covered my face. Unfortunately, that memory had been on repeat in my mind all night long.

Most of all, though, I kept thinking of the way his mood darkened so violently that I feared he would hit me. Had I imagined that part? The terrible tension in the air, the way his face had become so still and tight.

Why would mentioning Lisa make him so angry he wanted to hit me?

The truly screwed up part was that I honestly hadn't thought before I spoke. I wasn't trying to provoke him or anything like that. I was just thinking of weird stuff that had happened in this place. The whole thing with Lisa had always bothered me. In the back of my mind, I wondered if she had killed herself. It explained why no one ever wanted to talk about her. But now I didn't think that was the case since Becca said it had been years since the last suicide here.

I had to find Aaron and ask what his problem was, which was why I was waiting for him during rec. I just prayed he would walk in alone, so I could get him to talk to me.

I sat at a table, doodling in a sketchbook but mostly watching the door.

When Jon and Danny walked in, I froze. Aaron probably wasn't far behind.

I tried not to make eye contact with them so they wouldn't try to sit at my table. They breezed by, though—too caught up in whatever story Danny was telling to notice me.

Aaron walked in just a couple minutes later.

I hated how my heart seemed to skip at the sight of him. I had to remind myself of the dark expression he wore last night, the way his body had practically vibrated with tension. Before he could follow Jon and Danny to a table, I hurried over.

He looked at me with such a cold expression that I instinctively recoiled.

I wouldn't give up, though.

"I think it's time you finally told me what happened to Lisa," I said. "I didn't sleep at all last night because you freaked out on me at the mention of her."

"Are you just trying to screw with my head, or what?" he demanded in a low voice, eyes flashing.

"I'm just trying to find out the truth."

He laughed without humor at that. "Yeah, sure. Look, I can't waste any more time on you, okay? I need to focus on getting well and getting out of here."

I flinched and took another step back. "You act like I'm the one who kept approaching you. Everyone told me to stay away from you, and now I see why."

"It was a mistake, honestly. Feel free to take their advice and stay the fuck away from me." He started to walk away, but then he turned back. "And if you know what's good for you, you'll drop all this bullshit about supposed killings."

I wished I had come up with a better response than a venom-filled, "Asshole," as he left the room, but honestly, his sudden 180 had me reeling.

Now I was more suspicious than ever.

And I wished my friends had warned me that Aaron was obviously unstable. No one had said he would turn on me like a snake.

The burn of anger inside me had a bruised

quality to it, and I knew it would turn into hurt later. But for now, I held onto the feeling like a drowning person holds onto a life raft.

He accused me of trying to screw with his head, but he was clearly screwing with mine.

Maybe there was a reason he didn't want me going to Dr. Williams's office. Something more than simply worrying that I would get caught.

I didn't want to think that way—it made my heart twist painfully. I kept pushing the thought away, but it boomeranged back. Aaron. Lisa. Katelyn. Millie. What was the connection? What did it all mean?

I knew if I didn't find out, I really would lose my mind.

19

That night, we all had our tasks to complete to make the plan run smoothly. Jon would create a major diversion while Danny kept watch. Becca would steal the keys from the nurse's station, and I would break into the office. Aaron never showed up for our meeting during dinner to review the plan, and when the others asked why, I just played dumb. I didn't want to think about that right now. Besides, with Danny and Becca making sure the diversion was keeping the night staff busy, we didn't even need Aaron's help.

Now the four of us waited in one of the dark hallways closest to the nurse's station. I kept clenching and unclenching my fists to try and work off some of my anxiety. I couldn't afford to have a panic attack.

On night shift, only one nurse and two mental health techs kept watch. Tonight, Ethan patrolled the boys' hallway, and Cathy oversaw the girls. That was a stroke of good luck because both tended to wander away and go on excessive breaks. They weren't nearly as reliable as Jax. The nurse, though . . . when Becca saw who it was, she groaned.

"Denise is a stone-cold bitch," Becca said, "and worse, she doesn't spend all her time looking at her phone like the others. This is going to be ten times harder." She chewed her lip. "I don't know, maybe we should wait another night."

I tensed all over. "Even if my anxiety could handle that, Jon already set up his diversion."

Before Becca could respond, a small commotion drew our attention to the nurse's station. Ethan came striding toward Denise, a determined look on his face.

"Hey, I need you to call the cleanup crew, stat."

Denise just stared at him from above her reader glasses. She barely looked up from her book. "What are you talking about?"

"We've got a huge situation that needs cleaning. Huge. It's going to take them all night."

She regarded him like his stupidity knew no bounds. "There is no cleaning crew at night."

His mouth fell open. "What?"

She smirked at him. "*You* are the cleaning crew, and if it's a really big job, I suppose you can rope Cathy in to help."

Becca and I shared a look. We needed Nurse Denise to leave the station, too.

"You don't understand. This is a biohazard all over the stairs."

This got her attention. "What kind of biohazard?"

"Shit. All over the stairs."

Suddenly, Jon's comment from the night before made total sense. I tried not to laugh in surprise.

She heaved a sigh. "Not again." With what seemed like an enormous effort, she put her book down and stood up. "All right. Show me."

Becca had been watching closely, and the moment Nurse Denise went around the corner, she sprinted for the station.

With my heart in my throat, I watched for Nurse Denise to return. Becca made it there and back in about thirty seconds, no problem.

"That was the easy part," she said breathlessly. "Now let's get you to Williams's office before Nurse

Denise comes back. She won't stay away long. There's no way in hell she's cleaning up shit."

"Do I even want to know how Jon did that?" I asked with a disgusted shudder.

We continued past the nurse's station and to the main hallway where Dr. Williams's office was. Becca tried to handle the keys without jingling them, but there were too many on the keychain. She grabbed a large one that had a piece of tape on the end labeling it as the right one.

"Are they stupid or something?" I asked when I saw the helpful label.

"There are like thirty keys on this chain, and they don't expect us to steal them," she whispered back with a grin.

With one smooth movement, she opened the door with the key. We both winced when it squeaked loudly.

"Go as fast as you can," Becca said. "I'll keep watch by the nurse's station."

I slipped through the door but hesitated when it came to closing it again. I didn't want to risk that squeaky hinge, so I left it cracked open.

Very little light came from the doorway, but it provided enough to read by. The office seemed less tattered and old at night since I couldn't make out the details of the torn-up couch or the hideous paint choices.

The file cabinets lined one wall, and I went straight to them. When I pulled open the first one, a name jumped out at me: Aaron Jones. I ripped out the file. Maybe it would explain why he had lost his mind when it came to Lisa.

The first page contained his intake assessment and family history. At the very top, a stamp read, *Court Order.* Hungrily, I read the contents.

ROLLING GREEN PEDIATRIC MENTAL HEALTH FACILITY

Intake Assessment

Name: Aaron Jones

Date of Birth: 4/15/2005

Client Identification Number: 36-7898

REASON FOR REFERRAL

Aaron Jones was ordered by the court to receive at least 90 days of mental health treatment at this facility, under the care of Dr. Williams. This treatment was chosen over prison time due to Aaron's history of mental illness. In September,

Aaron assaulted another juvenile from his school in a vicious attack. Aaron waited for the other high school student in the parking lot and beat him until he was unconscious. The boy was hospitalized and remained in a comatose state for two days. When asked what started the fight, Aaron stated the other boy had "bullied him one too many times and needed to be taught a lesson."

Such an attack was not new for Aaron. He has gotten into multiple fights at school—at least once a week for verbal and once a month for physical. The school suspended him on numerous occasions, but this attack was his worst offense.

My hand holding the paper began to shake. Aaron was violent? Not only that, he had hurt another kid so bad it put him in a coma. I couldn't help thinking of the look he gave me last night. My instincts must have been right—maybe he really did want to hit me. He certainly had a history of it. I shook my head in disbelief. What else was he hiding?

I continued reading about his personal relationships.

Significant Personal Relationships

Aaron's father left his mother, his brother, and him

when he was ten years old. This has had a significant impact on Aaron because he blamed himself for his father's abandonment. He insists it's because of his mental health diagnosis. His older brother left just a few years after that to join the army. This only made Aaron's feelings of abandonment worse. He blamed himself for his older brother leaving just like he did with his father.

Aaron has no contact with his father, and very limited contact with his older brother. He has no living grandparents. His mother is his only family, but she can be emotionally neglectful due to her opioid addiction.

This lack of family guidance led Aaron to join a violent gang at the age of thirteen. Most of his peer-aged relationships are dysfunctional. He doesn't seem to trust anyone enough to confide in them, so he's often alone. Aaron is attracted to members of the opposite sex, but he rarely maintains relationships longer than a month. This isn't unusual for someone his age, but by his own admission, Aaron prefers to keep himself at a distance from others.

So what Aaron had told me about his father and brother had been true. Or, at least, he'd told the same thing to the counselors. The mention of him joining a violent gang had me chewing my bottom lip. It didn't fit with the Aaron I had seen most of the time here, but if I thought of the way he acted last night, it made sense.

History of Present Illness

Aaron was diagnosed with conduct disorder at the age of ten. His symptoms include violent and bullying behavior, vandalism, lying and manipulative behavior. As a teen, this diagnosis was revised to bipolar disorder as Aaron became more forthcoming with his symptoms of mania and depression. Many of his behaviors were found to be in response to gang-related pressure as well as a neglectful home life.

Aaron frequently engages in risk-taking behavior and tends to gravitate toward people who are toxic for him.

I reread that last line over and over, my heart twisting inside me. Was that why Aaron had been so persistent with me? Was I the toxic one? I kept reading, hoping to find the answer.

Current Symptoms

Aaron has difficulty controlling his anger and will often display fits of rage that are disproportionate to the catalyst. For example, he became so angry at being asked about his father during this assessment that he knocked the notepad out of the therapist's hand.

He reports anxiety, poor self-esteem, racing thoughts, and difficulty concentrating. He does acknowledge his anger management problems when confronted about them.

I thought about the way Aaron reacted so aggressively toward me when I asked about Lisa. This assessment made it sound like he had major anger issues. Maybe it wasn't really what I had said to him —maybe he just flew off the handle for any little thing. As much as I wanted to dig further and find out more about him, I couldn't waste any more time reading about Aaron. After skimming for the name Lisa but not finding it, I closed Aaron's file and shoved it back in the cabinet.

I glanced at the clock on the wall. Sweat beaded my hairline when I realized three minutes had already elapsed and I'd found basically nothing— other than proof my friends were right to warn me about Aaron.

A collage of framed articles from *Psychology Today* and other psychology journals hung on the wall beneath the clock. Sitting on the couch, I could never read them because of a glare from the overhead light. Now I could read the headlines clearly:

Psychiatrist Abram Williams Has 100% Success Rate with Violent Patients

Renowned Psychiatrist Is Leading Expert on Violent Patients

Psychiatrist Leads the Way with Treatment for Violence in the Mentally Ill

After reading Aaron's file, it made sense why he had been sent here. Apparently Dr. Williams was some kind of guru on violence. By the way the articles had all been framed, it seemed like he was proud of it, too.

I opened another drawer and scanned the names, skimming over the files with my fingertips to help me keep track. No Lisa in this one either. My heart beat faster when I realized that Katelyn's and Millie's were missing, too. It would help if I had anyone's last name, but we only knew each other by our first names—I guessed for privacy reasons.

All the files for the dead girls were missing. As I searched through the final drawer, I realized with a sickening sensation that my own file was missing. Cold fingers of fear traced down my spine.

What did it mean? Was I next?

Then I noticed a name filed under the current patients that I hadn't heard in group or anywhere else. *Emma Bryce.*

Emma by Jane Austen was one of my favorite novels, so I knew I would have remembered someone with that name.

So who was she?

I reached for the folder.

The door hinge squeaked, and I jerked my head in that direction just as Nurse Denise and Ethan walked into the room.

Heart pounding painfully in my chest, I tried to slip by them. As I did, Ethan grabbed hold of my arm. I screamed and tried to jerk away, but he held fast. He was smaller and wiry in frame compared to Jax, but he restrained me with ease.

"I thought I heard someone snooping in here," Nurse Denise said. "Not only are you breaking the safety rules of staying in your room at night, but you're also violating the privacy of the other residents."

"I had to find out what was going on here—why everyone is dying!"

"She sounds paranoid," Nurse Denise said to Ethan. "I think she's actively psychotic. We're going to have to put her in isolation until Dr. Williams gets here and can advise what to do."

Ethan started to drag me out of the office. I grabbed hold of the doorframe and refused to let go. He finally wrenched me free, and several of my nails broke painfully.

I kicked and thrashed, fighting him at every turn. Soon, Cathy came from the girl's hallway and helped drag me to a room I had never noticed before, not far from Dr. Williams's office.

Cathy opened the door, and I froze as I took in the wall-to-wall padding. I wrenched my arm away and took off down the hall again. I nearly succeeded in escaping, but Ethan outran me and grabbed hold of me again. I collapsed at the waist, sobbing as they dragged me into the room.

Cathy guarded the door as Ethan brought me all the way inside. He gave me a little push so that I stumbled, and then he dashed out of the room. Before I could chase after him, they closed the door in my face.

I pounded on it and rattled the knob, but it was locked firm against me.

I screamed again until tears pricked my eyes. The padded room absorbed the sound eerily, like being muffled underwater.

Images crowded my mind, and I grabbed either side of my head to make them stop.

They didn't want me to discover the truth about Katelyn and Millie. They had probably overheard something they shouldn't have and lost their lives for it. Now I'd been caught sneaking around in Dr. Williams's office, too.

Soon they would figure out I had help.

My teeth started chattering as a sickening feeling spread all over my body like a fever. It became hard to breathe. A cold sweat dotted my forehead and slipped down my back.

And I knew: we were all going to die.

20

I paced the room like a caged tiger, my anxiety whipping me on. My shoes made a rustling sound against the soft floor. Why did they think a room like this would calm someone down? Being surrounded by white padded walls made my blood rush in my veins. *I've got to get out of here,* I thought. *Get out, get out, get out.* Each thought echoed through my mind more desperately than the last. Outside the room, I couldn't hear anything. What had happened to Becca, Jon, and Danny? How did Nurse Denise and Ethan know I was in Dr. Williams's office?

They'll kill me to keep me silent, I thought, heart fluttering like a bird's wings.

No, that couldn't be right, the more logical side of me insisted. How could all the staff be in on the murders? How would you find that many evil people to be complicit in the murder of children?

Unless this place really was some weird cult.

I thought again of what I had seen in the file cabinets. Aaron had a violent past, so much that he barely avoided going to prison. He beat some kid until he was unconscious. Last night, his eyes had turned so cold at Lisa's name that I thought for one terrible minute he would hit me. I remembered the thrum of tension in the air, the way his body had hardened and his hands had become fists. Had he thought of hitting me? Lashing out to shut me up?

Katelyn had been willing to talk about Lisa. The others tried to warn her not to, but she did anyway. And now she was dead.

My mind raced to put it all together. A connection existed here, I just had to find it. Lisa. Katelyn. Millie.

Aaron?

Did Aaron do something to Lisa? Hurt her? *Kill* her?

A few days ago, I wouldn't have said it was possible. But then I saw the cold flash in his eyes, like a monster stirring just beneath the surface. A primal instinct inside me had responded, whispering that he wanted to hurt me.

Maybe Aaron killed Lisa, and Katelyn found out about it. That day she met with Dr. Williams, I thought she had been crying over something I said, but really, she could have just discovered the truth. All the others had been willing to forget about Lisa, but not her.

I could definitely see her trying to tell Dr. Williams about it, and he just called it distorted thinking or something.

Millie's connection was harder. She couldn't speak, so how could she be a threat? But then I thought about how she was so easily overlooked. She even hid around the hallway corner that time to eavesdrop without the techs knowing. The day of the snowfall, she suddenly started to speak, and Aaron was right there. He knew she'd broken her silence. Maybe Dr. Williams immediately brought her to his office to question her . . . to find out what really happened to Lisa.

I rubbed my forehead. No, that didn't make sense. If Lisa supposedly killed herself like the others, then Becca wouldn't have overheard the nurses saying it had been years since the last suicide here.

Unless she appeared to have died another way—in some sort of accident.

My heart pounded, my mouth ran dry.

And then when Katelyn and Millie discovered the truth . . .

He killed them?

And you let it happen, the mean voice inside me whispered. *Just like you did with your own sister.*

"No," I whispered thickly, tears filling my eyes.

I thought of Millie lying dead on the bathroom floor, her face frozen in fear. The nightmare of Katelyn being suffocated to death ran through my mind next, torturing me with the fact that I had advanced warning she would die.

I should have done something sooner. I had all the pieces of this puzzle—more than anyone else. I could have told Dr. Williams the truth, but I cared too much about what he thought about me. So what if he thought I was crazy? Didn't they already think that? I swallowed hard at the thought that Millie would still be alive if I hadn't been so self-absorbed.

But the dreams and bad feeling I had ignored weren't the only ways I was responsible for their deaths. I also kept mentioning Lisa, continually, even when I knew it stirred the pot. I spoke about her to my friends who told me to stop bringing her up, to Dr. Williams, and worst of all, to Aaron.

And he had killed to keep them all silent.

Now I had dragged Becca, Danny, and Jon into it. Aaron knew they suspected Millie and Katelyn had been murdered. My breaths came faster when I realized I couldn't warn them. They were out there, completely unsuspecting of Aaron.

I could see it all in my mind.

He would approach them one by one. Jon slept in the same room with him, so all he had to do was wait for tonight. Until he was asleep. And then what? Strangle him like I saw in my dream? Hang him from the light fixture so it looked like another suicide by hanging?

My heart ached for how devastated Danny would be. Would Danny start to figure it out then?

I paused in my frantic pacing. Or maybe Aaron wouldn't want to take a chance on them letting me out of here and telling everyone the truth. Maybe he would just kill them all now.

What if they finally let me out of here, and all my friends were dead . . . because of me?

I ran to the door and pounded on it with my fists. The padding absorbed the blows, so I shouted.

"Let me out of here! I have to warn them!"

But of course no one came. I sounded like a paranoid psychotic person.

I shouted until my throat hurt. The minutes turned into an hour, and still no one came. Sobbing, I curled up in a ball in the corner of the room.

My temperature fluctuated from hot to cold, and I broke out in a sweat. My teeth chattered like I had been plunged into the middle of a snowstorm.

I didn't need to dream of their deaths to know my friends were in danger.

And it was all my fault.

<hr>

What felt like hours later, I scrambled to my feet when I heard the rattling of keys at the door. I froze as it opened. But instead of Nurse Denise or the techs, Becca rushed in.

I nearly collided with her as I wrapped my arms around her in a tight hug. Immediately, tears fell as I struggled to convey everything in one garbled sentence. "Thank God you're here . . . Aaron's the one. You were right—we gotta get out of here—who will even help us?"

Becca gently disentangled herself from me and steered me out of the room. Danny and Jon waited in the hallway.

"We're so sorry you got caught," Danny said, looking grim. "None of us could figure out what set them off. One minute, the techs were scrubbing shit, the next, that bitchy nurse was demanding they come with her."

"I had to wait until they left before breaking you out of here," Becca said, holding up the keys. "What were you saying about Aaron?"

"I think Aaron's the killer," I said in a rush. "And I think we're next."

Danny paled and Jon looked stunned. Becca just muttered, "I fucking knew it."

"You saw something in Dr Williams's office, then?" Jon asked.

"I saw enough to put it all together. We gotta get out of here."

"We need to go to the police," Danny said.

"And say what?" Becca said. "We're in a mental institution and we think someone is trying to kill us? Yeah, they'll come running."

"What about telling Dr. Williams?" Danny said. "He can't call us all delusional!"

I thought of Katelyn and Millie going to his office and leaving upset. Had they tried to get help from him, too?

A painful headache throbbed behind my eyes. I didn't know what we could do.

"Let's get out of here," Becca said. "We'll figure the rest out when we're safe."

The best way out would be one of the side entrances in the rear of the facility, where deliveries were made. We would have to go past the nurse's station again, but Nurse Denise probably wasn't there anymore. Most likely, she was patrolling the halls.

For us.

Becca took off at a run, and we followed. The breaths burst out of me, my lungs burning. Every instinct in my body screamed that we had to hurry, or we would be next. Suicided just like poor Katelyn and Millie.

We tried to run quietly, but our shoes pounded on the vinyl flooring. Our scrubs made loud swishing sounds. We stopped just before the hallway fed out into the main entryway, where the nurse's station was. Nurse Denise wasn't anywhere to be seen.

Becca signaled that we'd have to go back through the main hall. It was the only way to reach the back hallway that led to the rear service entrance. Danny and I shared matching wide-eyed looks. Goose-bumps covered my arms as blood rushed in my veins.

Becca started first, sneaking quietly and slowly to begin with, but then picking up speed as she got to the middle of the hall. I did the same, holding my breath the whole time. Danny and Jon brought up the rear, their footsteps echoing behind mine.

Everything in me said, *Don't get caught again*. I couldn't go back into that padded room.

Just before we could reach the back hallway, Nurse Denise stepped out of it and blocked our path. She scowled at us, her cheeks bright red from exertion.

"Nobody move!" she shouted.

Used to following the nursing staff's orders, we froze. My breaths came in a panted rush. Danny looked at Jon, and I looked at Becca. Her jaw tightened with determination.

"Fuck that!" Becca yelled and shoved her out of the way, hard enough that she hit the wall.

As we hurried past, I heard Nurse Denise use her walkie talkie to contact the others. "Code Brown," she shouted into it. "They're in the back hallway that leads to the rear service entrance."

Danny whimpered behind me. We might not know exactly what would happen to us if we got caught now, but it couldn't be good.

We ran like flesh-eating monsters chased us, the hallway dark and silent. With my senses heightened from the rush of adrenaline, I could hear every panicked breath my friends took. I smelled the mustiness beneath the chemical scent of disinfectants used to clean the floor. I felt the beads of sweat track down my spine.

As we rounded the corner, two figures stood in our way.

Dr. Williams and Aaron.

Our jaws dropped. Aaron stood beside Dr. Williams like he was one of the mental health techs, there to apprehend us. He regarded us coldly, without an ounce of sympathy on his face. And I realized: he must have been the one to tell Nurse Denise I was in Dr. Williams's office tonight. He was the only other one who knew about the plan.

I had a sudden memory of his warning last night —about the padded room. He knew what would happen to me if I got caught, but he told them anyway.

"You got me thrown in isolation," I said, incredulousness making my voice sound higher than it usually did.

He gave me this look like, *I warned you.*

Jon stepped forward. "Dude, you ratted us out?"

Aaron didn't even bother to respond.

Seeing him standing there with Dr. Williams made the final pieces click in my head. I thought of the framed articles on the wall, the obvious pride Dr. Williams took in being an expert on violent patients. No doubt he took Aaron on expecting to rehabilitate him like all the others. But Aaron was different. He must have killed Lisa and made it look like an accident. Maybe Dr. Williams suspected the truth. Maybe he thought he could still do something about it. But then Aaron killed Katelyn and Millie, too. Dr.

Williams had to cover it all up to protect his reputation. How would everyone in his field react if they knew he not only failed to help Aaron, but had allowed him free enough rein to kill three of his fellow patients?

The only question was: what did Dr. Williams plan to do now that he knew we had figured it out?

"You're in on it together," I said slowly. "Aaron couldn't have staged those deaths on his own. He needed help." To the others, I said, "Dr. Williams would apparently do anything to protect his reputation as an expert on rehabilitating violent patients. Even if it means making murders look like suicides."

Danny made a strangled sound in his throat and Jon grabbed his hand while keeping his eyes on Aaron, his expression a mask of fury. Even Becca's face appeared leeched of color.

"How could you listen to her?" Aaron demanded. "She's obviously out of her mind."

"Sadie's not the one standing over there next to Dr. Williams like he's ready to come drag us off to the padded room," Jon snapped.

"How could you hurt Millie?" Becca asked, her voice pained. "How could you do that to her?"

"I think we've heard enough," Dr. Williams said. "Aaron informed me of your, frankly psychotic, plan.

You all need to come with me now to have a little talk."

No one moved.

"Millie obviously saw something she shouldn't have," Aaron said, and I stared at him in a horrified stupor. That was exactly what I thought happened. "Once she started to talk, that was the end of her."

Becca let out a frustrated growl and launched herself at Aaron, who shoved her back before her hand could connect with his face.

Dr. Williams shouted at them to stop and moved to put himself in the middle of the fight. I grabbed hold of Becca's arm and tugged her back beside me just as Jon attacked Aaron. They traded punches, the sound of connecting flesh echoing in the hall. Dr. Williams got knocked aside in the chaos.

Once he righted himself, he marched toward us, a grim determination on his face. "You have to come with me now."

Then we heard a horrible crack, and Jon slumped to the floor. He lay there without moving, blood trickling from his mouth.

We all stared at each other, unable to fully comprehend the situation in front of us. How hard did Aaron hit him? A line from the assessment I read in Dr. Williams's office floated through my mind: . . . *beat him until he was unconscious* . . . *hospitalized and remained in a comatose state for two days.*

Danny screamed.

This seemed to snap us out of our shock. Aaron moved toward us threateningly.

"Run!" Becca yelled, and we all scattered.

21

Like one of my nightmares, I ran down the dimly lit hallway. Blood rushed in my ears as my heart pounded violently. Aaron and Dr. Williams may have been behind us, but I had no idea where Nurse Denise and the two mental health techs had gone. I jumped at every shadow as I ran for the closest place to hide: the kitchen. I could regroup there and figure out how to get out of here alive. I didn't have a plan beyond that. I had the mentality of a hunted animal: keep running. Stay alive.

I raced past the nurse's station without pausing. It seemed empty. My skin crawled like I was in a horror film waiting on a jump scare. I hadn't stayed around to listen, but Dr. Williams most likely radioed ahead for the staff to find us and lock us up.

Suddenly, pounding footsteps behind me echoed through the hallway.

"Sadie!" Aaron yelled. "Come out here, you psycho."

Underneath my panicked fear of being chased, a sliver of rage pierced my heart. What the hell was his problem? Did he plan to kill us all? Would Dr. Williams help? I thought of Jon, lying on the floor with blood coming from his mouth. We hadn't even checked to make sure he was still breathing.

My heart strained against my rib cage as I finally reached the kitchen. I wrenched open the door and tumbled inside.

Someone had turned off even the dim light above the stove, so darkness filled the room. I walked carefully with my arm outstretched, trying to find the island so I could get my bearings.

The soft sound of a shoe on linoleum froze me in place. I twitched like a rabbit, my hand touching the wooden base. Cabinets lined one side of the island, I remembered, but they were filled with pots and pans. It would make far too much noise if I tried to hide there.

The door opened, and I crouched down on the

side of the island across from it. A light switched on, illuminating everything in the room. I tried not to whimper.

All the person had to do was come around the island and I would be spotted. I would have to crawl around it, always keeping the countertop between me and my pursuer.

Steady footsteps brought the person closer to where I hid. Holding my breath, I crawled toward the side closest to the stove.

The shoe-on-linoleum sound grew quieter until finally it stopped. Had they left? Or were they waiting for me to reveal myself? My legs shook while I crouched there, terrified to move.

When the door clicked shut, I had a desperate urge to peek around the side of the island, but I didn't dare.

I counted slowly to thirty in my head before finally risking it. Shifting my weight little by little, I crawled toward the corner of the island so I could see the door.

A hand landed on my ankles and pulled.

I screamed and kicked out with both legs, but he held tight to them. Expecting Aaron, I jolted with surprise to see Dr. Williams instead.

"We're just going to go somewhere to calm down, Sadie," he said, dragging me toward him.

I threw a punch at Dr. Williams but succeeded only in knocking off his glasses. He snarled at me in frustration, more emotion than I'd ever seen from him. Stronger than he looked, he held me down easily. As I struggled, I saw him pull something black and vaguely gun-shaped from his pocket.

Cold dread poured over me like ice water. I fought against him with renewed energy, loosening his hold on my legs. I wouldn't just sit here and let him murder me.

I succeeded in getting one leg free and kicked out.

With gritted teeth, he brought the hand with the gun toward me.

Becca appeared behind him, holding a heavy pan. She crashed it down over his head. Abruptly, he released his hold on me and toppled over. Stunned.

"Becca, thank God," I said, my voice coming out in a panted rush.

"Quit thanking God and get up," she said, hauling me to my feet. "We need to leave."

"Wait." I hurried over to the drawers. It took me several tries before I found one, but then I held the chef's knife up for her to see. The blade glinted in the light.

She nodded with approval. "We'll head for the main entrance."

We ran out the kitchen door and down the long hallway, past the dining room and rec room. Breathing hard, our footsteps reverberating like gunshots in my ears, we burst out into the entryway near the nurse's station again.

That's when we heard Danny yell.

"We have to help him!" I told Becca.

She had stopped to listen, eyes wide. Ultimately, she shook her head. "No way. I only stopped to help you because   "

She cut herself off, and I stared at her. "What? You just happened to be going that way anyway?"

Her expression turned sheepish. "I was running from Ethan. He thought I went the direction Danny is screaming from now."

I couldn't stop to dwell on the fact that she hadn't even really wanted to help me.

I grabbed hold of her arm. "We're not leaving Danny behind in this murder house."

Becca hesitated, and I stared her down. "Fine," she said, her breath coming out in a rush.

Danny screamed again, and I raced in that direction, Becca on my heels.

Our feet pounded down the hallway, but just before I could round the corner, Becca grabbed my sleeve and hauled me back.

"What?" I hissed, but she put a finger to her lips.

The sounds of a fight echoed down the next hallway.

We peered around the corner at them. Aaron had his back to us with Danny up against the wall, handfuls of his scrub top in both fists. Danny grabbed both of Aaron's arms, but he clearly didn't have the strength to fight back. Danny's face had turned bright red from the effort of keeping Aaron from choking him. I moved toward them, but Becca held out her arm and shook her head at me.

Aaron shoved him again. "Where is she?" he demanded. "Where's Sadie?"

"I don't know!" Danny said in a strangled voice. "We all split up."

"Why does he want you?" Becca whispered.

I shook my head with wide eyes. Whatever the reason, it couldn't be good.

"I'll distract him," Becca said quietly. "You help Danny."

She jumped out from behind the corner and shouted at Aaron, "Let him go."

I listened hard from my hiding spot, tightening my grip on the knife as I waited for my chance to come to Danny's rescue. My palms were slick with sweat.

The sounds of grunting and shoes squeaking loudly on linoleum rang out, and I raced out from behind the corner. Becca had drawn Aaron's attention and forced him to let go of Danny. As Aaron stalked toward her, Danny jumped at his back. Aaron turned to face Danny again, so he never saw me. I didn't take time to think. I ran forward, knife at my side.

I launched myself at Aaron's broad back. Before he could turn around, I slipped my arm around his neck from behind. The edge of the knife just barely touched his skin.

He froze.

Becca held out her hand to Danny, and he raced to join her.

"I trusted you, Aaron," I told him, my heart thudding painfully in my chest as I shifted to one side. "How could you do this?"

"You're the one with a knife at my throat," he said. Cocky words, but I felt his Adam's apple bob against the blade.

"Why did you kill them?" I asked. "What did either of them ever do to you?"

"I didn't kill anyone," he growled.

I pressed the blade harder against his neck until small beads of blood welled up.

"Stop!" a voice shouted down the hallway.

We turned to see Dr. Williams hurrying toward us, both hands wrapped around a gun.

"Drop the knife."

I gripped the knife handle harder, so no one would see my hands shake. Dr. Williams pointed the gun at me, chilling my blood down to my marrow. I had never even seen a gun in real life, despite living in Georgia where practically everyone I knew had at least one. I never imagined I would have one pointed at my head.

Danny and Becca had matching expressions of

terror as they watched helplessly from where they'd huddled together against the wall.

"Back up," I shouted, pressing the knife to Aaron's throat hard enough to make him wince. "I'll kill him, I swear," I threatened. The thought of continuing to slice the knife into his neck until he bled freely, until he died, made my vision swim. I thought I might faint.

Dr. Williams continued to train the gun on me.

"Holding a gun on your own patients makes you look like the psycho," I said.

"I'm protecting one patient from another," he said, using that annoyingly calm psychiatrist voice again.

"It wouldn't have gotten to this point if the two of you hadn't killed our friends and covered it up!" I yelled.

"That never happened, Sadie."

Frustration lit a fire inside me. "There's no point in lying! We know they weren't suicides."

"No, they weren't."

Silence filled the hallway as we all stared at Dr. Williams.

Becca spoke up. "Then you knew . . . you knew they had been killed?"

"Katelyn and Millie were killed," he said calmly, almost regretfully. "Though it looked like suicide."

Confusion had my mind in knots. He had confirmed what I suspected—that they had been killed, and the attacker made it look like suicide. But then why were he and Aaron chasing us down, acting like they wanted to kill us? If they didn't do it, who did?

He had mentioned Katelyn and Millie, but there was another patient here whose mystery I wanted to finally solve.

"And what about Lisa?" I asked. "Did someone kill her, too?"

Becca whipped her head toward me, and Danny looked at me strangely. "Lisa?" Becca repeated with an incredulous tone. "You think Lisa is dead?"

"I don't know what happened to her," I said. "That's the point. I think she was killed, though, just like the others."

Becca looked at me like I was another species. She glanced at Danny, like he might better explain the situation. He shook his head.

Her expression turned to pity. Very slowly, Becca said, "Sadie, Lisa doesn't exist."

22

___

Ice hit my veins, and my stomach plummeted. I took a step back, my arm dropping away from Aaron's neck. He walked away slowly without taking his eyes off me, like you would move in the presence of a wolf.

"What do you mean she doesn't exist?" I asked, my voice sounding hesitant.

Whispers ran through my mind that I shouldn't listen to whatever they had to say. That this was all one big conspiracy, designed to hurt me. The whispers sounded very far away, but I knew if I concentrated, they would be louder.

For a moment, I almost gave in just so all of this would go away. I knew I made certain decisions that led me down this path, where Aaron's neck bled from the knife I wielded, and Dr. Williams pointed a gun on me. The whispers in my mind tempted me into disappearing within the safety of my subconscious.

But I couldn't do that. Not again. I wanted to hear the truth.

When I lowered the knife, Dr. Williams lowered his gun, too, but I noticed he didn't put it away.

"Sadie, you have dissociative identity disorder," Dr. Williams said. "Do you know what that means?"

A memory floated to the top of my conscious mind of being in a doctor's office with my mother, both of us seated across from a balding psychiatrist with thick glasses. "I'm sorry to say your daughter has all the signs of dissociative identity disorder," he said with a slight Indian accent. "This condition is often exacerbated by trauma. Do you know what trauma she may have experienced?" My mother had looked at me, but the memory just disappeared after that. I couldn't summon another second of it; some force within me shoved it back down. A mental block remained.

"No," I said.

"The diagnosis used to be called multiple personality disorder, but it was renamed to try to give a more accurate description of what the person experiences. It's both very rare and hard to define."

"I have a severe anxiety disorder and PTSD," I said, shaking my head. "I don't have whatever dissociations are." I looked to my friends for help, but they watched me with unreadable expressions.

"Anxiety is one of the symptoms, and DID can occur after severe childhood trauma," he said in calm tones that made me grit my teeth. "Dissociations are when your mind tries to protect you from whatever it finds upsetting emotionally by disconnecting you from reality. So you may find you have gaps in your memory or frequently experience a surreal, dream-like state."

I thought of the way I couldn't remember anything before my parents dropped me off, or how even my sister's death had largely disappeared from my memory. Trauma made you forget, though. It wasn't like I forgot big parts of my day or anything.

"In the case of DID, you dissociate to the point that your consciousness creates new, alternate personalities. Remember when I said the mind was an incredible thing? It's powerful enough to create alters with their own distinct likes and dislikes, backgrounds, and emotions." He leveled his gaze at me, and it felt like I was staring into the abyss. "Do you understand what I'm saying to you?"

The whispers in my head began to clamor all at once, and for some reason, I looked at Aaron.

"You are Lisa, Sadie," he said, and it felt like a wave crashed over my head. I grasped hold of my chest. I couldn't breathe.

"Dr. Williams said we couldn't tell you," Becca said with a glance at the doctor, her eyes narrowed slightly. "He said it would only upset you and slow down your progress."

Danny spoke up from beside Becca, his expression still incredulous. "We never would have gone along with all this if we had known you thought that about Lisa. You never said you thought she had been killed along with Millie and Katelyn. We just wanted to find out the truth."

"We believed you when you said their deaths seemed suspicious," Becca said, her tone becoming sharper, "but we didn't realize you had it all wrong. We didn't know you thought Lisa was dead, too."

If it had just been Dr. Williams telling me, then I wouldn't have believed him. But the fact that Becca, Danny, and even Aaron said Lisa didn't exist hit me so hard my mind struggled to keep up.

The beautiful but disturbing sketch I saw in art floated through my thoughts, drawn by Lisa. Drawn by me? All those faces . . . I had thought they were different emotions, but now I realized the drawing could also be interpreted as alternate personalities.

"Your birth name is Emma Bryce," Dr. Williams said, and immediately I thought of the file I found in his office—the one I had almost pulled out and read. "Lisa and Sadie are alters your mind created to protect you from the truth."

No, my mind said, *don't ask this.*

"What truth?" I asked.

"Let's go back to my office and discuss this," he said, gesturing to me with the hand not holding a deadly weapon. "This isn't the place to hear about your trauma."

"I'm not going anywhere with you," I snapped. "In case you forgot, two girls are dead. Now, tell me about this truth you think I don't know."

He hesitated.

"Tell me!" I shouted so loudly the others jumped.

"Amber wasn't the only one to die in the fire. Your parents are dead, too."

I nearly dropped the knife. "No," I said in a pained groan. "No, I remember them bringing me here."

"Sadie remembers that, but it was a hallucination. A memory fabricated by your mind to protect you from the truth."

I thought of Aaron and me, sitting alone during the family visitation day. Of waiting and waiting for my parents to arrive. I would never see them again.

I tried to picture their faces, but nothing came to mind. I couldn't even remember their names. A sick feeling washed over me, and my heart raced. Why couldn't I remember them?

My mind cracked then, like hairline fractures on a ceramic bowl. If what Dr. Williams said was true, then who was I? Did I really love art? Was I bullied by my family for being crazy like I thought? Was my bedroom even the way I remembered it?

What made me, *me*?

Becca spoke up then, her hands in fists at her sides. "We get that we got caught up in——" she waved her hand toward me, "whatever is going on with Sadie, but we know something happened to Millie and Katelyn. And it wasn't suicide."

Danny pulled her back to his side, away from Dr. Williams and Aaron, and close to the wall. He clearly didn't trust them either. "We just want to know the truth. We want to know what happened to our friends."

Becca's cheeks flushed under her deep tan, and her eyes flashed a warning as she stared down Dr. Williams. "Earlier you said you knew they weren't suicides, so I guess I'm curious as to why the *fuck* you haven't called the police yet."

"That's because I didn't put it all together until it was too late, and I still don't know what happened here," Dr. Williams said, his face drawn. He turned his attention to me. "We were hoping you could explain, Sadie. Emma has never had a violent alter before."

The hairline cracks widened until my mind split open, images and memories pouring out like water.

Dr. Williams, Aaron, and all the others faded away as I lost my grip on reality. I disappeared inside myself. Deep within my mind, I walked down a long, dark hallway. Light spilled out from a room at the end of it. I shook at the thought of going in there, but at the same time, I knew I had to. I would finally find out the truth. The closer I got to the room, the more the walls around me trembled, as though they would collapse.

I walked through the door, my heart in my throat. A giant movie theater screen took up one wall. A single seat faced the screen.

I froze, but some unseen force pushed me

forward. Reluctantly, I sat down. I squeezed my eyes closed, unwilling to see whatever was about to play on the screen.

It played anyway, and my eyelids refused to stay shut.

The memory that played was like one of my prophetic nightmares, only this time, I could see the figure clearly.

Her reddish-blonde hair hung in a stringy sheet down her back, and she wore an oversized T-shirt and jeans. She turned, and I saw the smattering of freckles across her cheeks. Whole-some. She didn't look like someone about to light her own house on fire with her family inside.

There was no denying the girl was me.

That night, while my family slept, I poured accelerant all over the furniture and carpet on the first floor, up the stairs, and throughout the hallways on the second floor. The carpet and rugs soaked up the gasoline like a sponge. The smell of it filled my nostrils, obliterating the scent of my mother's air fresheners. By some miracle, the stench didn't wake any of them up.

I looked down at my hand on one of the red gas tanks, at the familiar pattern of freckles. This was my hand, though I couldn't completely access my thoughts and emotions at the time. Why did I do this? What made me decide to kill my family? Was my true identity just a psychopath?

As Sadie, I could easily tell you how I felt. My heart raced in my chest as I watched helplessly, horror and a deep sadness threatening to tear me apart.

But this girl who had sprinkled gasoline so methodically all over her family's house . . . I didn't know her.

I stood outside my parents' bedroom. From inside my jeans pocket, I took out a cheap motel matchbook. Without hesitation, I lit it and threw the match inside. I turned and ran as the fire spread, the flames licking hungrily everywhere the gas had spilled. I made it to the stairs and didn't wait to see how much damage I left behind.

I yanked open the front door, and before I ran outside, I heard the screams.

"No," I moaned now, holding my head. "Please tell me it's not true."

Distantly, I could hear Dr. Williams's voice, trying to pull me back to the present. Slowly, I became aware of my surroundings again. Of Dr. Williams watching me closely, of my friends unable to look me in the eyes. I couldn't bear to see it. A sob escaped my throat, and I covered my face.

"Focus, Sadie," he said. "Stay here with us."

"I can't," I said.

"What happened to Katelyn and Millie?" Dr. Williams pressed.

Against my will, I sank back into the depths of my subconscious mind.

I returned to that same room, only a different memory played on the screen. *I let out a panicky sound as I recognized the girls' bathroom at the mental facility. A girl who looked like me—though I had no memory of it as Sadie—hid behind the bathroom door. I peeked out at the hallway, where Cathy, the mental health tech walked past.*

As soon as Cathy started down the stairs, I left the bathroom and hurried down the hall. When I came to the third door past my own, I quietly pulled it open and slipped inside. In the bed on the right side of the room, Katelyn slept soundly. I checked the other side of the room, but her roommate's bed was empty. I remembered that her roommate had been sick that day and spent the night in the sick room, or running to the bathroom to puke.

I crept over to Katelyn's side of the bed and stared down at her in a disturbed silence. As with my memories of my parents, I had no access to the thoughts and memories going through my head at the time. I couldn't remember even leaving my room that night, much less creeping into Katelyn's room. When I tried to think of why I would do such a thing, my mind came up blank. I didn't know the reason behind the attack. I cried out inwardly, watching my past self reach out and grab hold of Katelyn's slim neck. I felt like a prisoner forced to watch a horrifying murder, like my eyes had been taped open.

Katelyn's arms flailed, trying to grab hold of the hands choking the life out of her. Her eyes seemed impossibly large as her face changed colors. She bucked and kicked, but she couldn't dislodge me. The more she fought, the more she used up the oxygen her body so desperately needed. She punched my back and scratched. It hurt, but I ignored the pain. I held on as she continued to struggle. Soon, her punches grew weaker.

Eventually, her arms fell to her sides. Her movement stopped.

I stayed there for another minute, and then I let go. A blood vessel had popped in her eye, turning it red. Her mouth stayed open, like a silent scream.

After carefully checking the hallway for Cathy again, I left the room and returned to my own.

This memory and my dream were nearly identical. I just hadn't realized I had been the one smothering her. But why had they told us she had hanged herself from her light fixture? Had someone covered this up?

"Sadie, what happened to Katelyn?" Dr. Williams said, and I tried to focus on his voice. The room with the screen faded for a moment.

Danny's eyes narrowed at me, but at the same time, tears filled them. I could only imagine what he felt toward me right then.

I retreated into myself just as another memory played across the screen.

This time of Millie.

---

*N*o, *I can't watch this,* I thought, trying to push the memory away. It didn't matter that my mind teetered on the edge of a precipice, about to fall and shatter into a million pieces. It just continued to roll through the images, like a movie I couldn't shut off.

I lay awake on my bed, waiting for the moment when Millie went to the bathroom. Every night, in the middle of the night, she got up to go. Weak bladder or something.

A few moments later, she woke up and crawled out of bed. She padded quietly over to the door.

It closed quietly behind her.

That's when I got out of bed and grabbed the piece of glass I had hidden in my desk drawer. Last time I had been in the kitchen for Katelyn's memorial, I had noticed a cabinet with drinking glasses. I went back one night and broke the glass until I had a long, jagged shard.

Holding my makeshift weapon, I followed her to the bathroom. Silence filled the hallway. Everyone else slept unaware, and the tech on night shift had wandered off as usual. I slipped into the bathroom without a sound.

Millie had just come out of one of the stalls when she saw me come in. She smiled at me in greeting. But then the smile fell away.

There must have been something in my expression, something threatening. She took one look at me and darted toward the door. I blocked her way.

No, no, I thought as Sadie, *I can't watch this. Not Millie. Please.*

But my mind was like a cruel torturer. Completely deaf to my pleas.

I grabbed hold of Millie. She tried to fight back, but she couldn't even push me off her. I caught hold of one skinny wrist and sliced it open. She opened her mouth to scream, but no sound escaped. She still couldn't speak on demand. Not even to save her life.

Blood rushed down her arm. I sliced the other, as easily as filleting a fish. She sank slowly to the floor. I helped lay her down, arms outstretched. I left the bloody glass beside her.

I watched until she lost consciousness, and then I left.

No, I whimpered. It was unimaginable that I had done such a thing.

I knew the rest. I would return to my bed and have a nightmare about Millie's death. Later I would find her in the bathroom.

A scream built inside me, and I knew if I released it, I would never stop.

"Millie," I sobbed.

"Did you kill Millie, Sadie?" Dr. Williams asked, his voice pulling me out of the room with the memory screen.

I came back to myself in the hallway, with everyone staring at me. Becca and Danny wore a mixture of fear and horror on their faces. Aaron looked at me with disgust. Dr. Williams struggled to maintain a neutral expression, but he was failing.

Tears streamed down my face. "Oh God, I killed them all."

23

The realization that I murdered people and didn't even know it tore my mind apart. I screamed and pulled my hair as the others looked on with disturbed expressions. I was beyond caring, though. Everything I thought I knew about myself was a lie. Dr. Williams said I didn't even exist. Emma Bryce had made me up as an alternate personality.

The pain of this realization grew so unbearable that I had to dissociate from it. Like a balloon suddenly cut free from its tether, I let go. My body remained behind, still in the hallway facing Dr. Williams and my former friends.

I returned to that long hallway in my mind. The room with the screen that projected my memories had disappeared. In its place, a lake with deep, dark water beckoned me. Fog moved across the surface as gentle waves lapped at the pebbled shore. I walked toward it with the intention of going in as deep as I could and sinking under the water.

Smooth pebbles massaged my bare feet as I made way closer to the shoreline. At the edge of the water, I stopped. A thought flitted through my mind:

I had no recollection of the thoughts and emotions that led up to killing my family and fellow patients here. As Sadie, I never would have done such a thing.

Then who had?

I did, a voice said deep in the recesses of my brain. A very male voice.

Time seemed to stop. *Who are you?* I asked inwardly.

In the lake in the middle of my subconscious mind, something struggled to the surface. The deep, dark water rippled as it became displaced by someone rising from the bottom. I stared harder, but I couldn't quite make out a form yet. The air around me shimmered with tension, and the foggy lake took on a sinister quality. I knew instinctively that this personality was dangerous. Letting him out could be devastating for everyone standing in the hallway.

I'm Zach, he said, *and I've watched you screw things up for Emma long enough.*

Bubbles came from the center of the lake as he rose higher from its depths.

I stumbled away from the shoreline, scrambling on the rocks. If this personality was responsible for the deaths of not only my family, but Katelyn and Millie as well, I had to do all I could to keep him from taking control.

I held out both my hands. *Stay there.*

He began to emerge, his face just barely detectable under the surface of the water. I tried to focus on the sensations outside of my body. Maybe if I had a better grip on reality, he wouldn't be able to take over.

The stuffy air of the hallway enveloped me as I opened my eyes and focused on the faces of my friends.

Becca's lip curled when our eyes met, and I hastily averted my gaze.

Inside my mind, Zach caused the waves of the lake to grow stronger, drawing my attention away from the hallway again.

"You can't come out," I said, clenching my jaw and using all my inner power to hold him back. I tried to maintain my hold on Emma's mind.

Dr. Williams gestured for the others to move farther away. "Sadie, who are you talking to?"

You can't handle this situation, Zach told me, *and you're just going to get Emma locked up again. It's time I took care of things.*

"No, I won't let you have control," I said in a growl. I shook all over from the effort to restrain him. My vision kept flashing back and forth from the scene in front of me to the one that existed only in my subconscious. "You'll hurt them."

Damn right I will. I'm the only one with the balls to do it.

Dr. Williams grimaced with concern. "Sadie, you have to stay in control. Don't let this alter come through."

I tried to listen to Dr. Williams, but Zach continued to surface no matter what I did. Soon, I could see him about to break through the deep lake at the center of Emma's subconscious.

"Who is it?" Dr. Williams asked with a sense of urgency in his tone. "What is the alter's name?"

"Zach," I said, my control slipping further. "He's the killer."

I could only see the lake and hear Dr. Williams and the others distantly. Dr. Williams tried to encourage me to fight back, but his voice faded out completely. I couldn't answer.

In that moment, Zach stepped out of the lake of Emma's subconscious mind. He appeared before me, tall and strong, with dripping wet hair. Malevolence emanated from him in waves. I couldn't help but cringe before him. In this surreal place, he seemed large as a giant. I didn't know how to send him back to where he came from, and I had the immediate sense I wasn't strong enough to do it. He had hidden himself from me this whole time, even as he murdered my family and friends. I thought of Becca, Danny, and Aaron now.

Please don't hurt them.

He took his wide palm and placed it on my head. With a sneer, he shoved me hard.

I flew through the air, weightless as though we were on the moon. As I sailed backward, I saw Emma, curled up peacefully on a brightly colored bed filled with pillows.

Emma! I shouted. *Wake up! You're the only one who can get control of him now. Call him back!*

But she slept on, oblivious as Sleeping Beauty.

Around me, the stone walls of a well rose up out of nowhere. I tried to grab hold of the side, but whatever power Zach had forced me down until I tumbled to the bottom with a pained grunt and looked back up.

Only a small circle of light came down from the very top of the well. The rest of it was plunged into darkness, and I couldn't even see my hand in front of my face. I could picture what I looked like, frantic and wild-eyed at the bottom of a dark well. The light penetrated only a few inches at the very top. With dawning horror, I realized it was just like my painting. The one that had disturbed Jon.

And now I was as trapped as the girl in the drawing.

24

Dr. Williams

Even in the midst of such a dangerous situation, the drastic changes that occurred to a person when an alter took over never ceased to amaze me. When Zach assumed control of Emma, every trace of sadness and angst disappeared from her face, leaving behind a cold mask. Even her posture changed. Her arms had dropped to her sides, and now she stood tall, legs slightly apart. She watched us with an unflinching, hard gaze.

I took a step forward, so the kids were behind

me. My heart raced in my chest. This was a situation that could rapidly get out of control, and I didn't want to endanger them. At the same time, telling them to run might cause Emma to attack. I kept one hand on the butt of the gun I had in the back of my pants. I didn't want to use it, but I would if I had to. Emma still had a knife.

"Are you Zach?" I asked.

"Yes," Emma/Zach replied, her voice pitched much lower than Sadie's had been.

"Are you responsible for Katelyn's and Millie's deaths?"

"I am Emma's protector, and I will take out any threat."

"What?" Becca said angrily from behind me. "How could Katelyn and Millie be a threat to you?"

I held out my hand to silence her. The last thing we needed was for this alter to feel threatened.

"Katelyn couldn't keep her mouth shut."

This time Danny bristled. "What's that supposed to mean?"

Zach's cold gaze zeroed in on Danny. "Katelyn wasn't afraid to talk about Lisa. She would have eventually told Sadie the truth, and I couldn't let her find out."

"Find out what?" I asked.

"That she isn't alone. That there are other alters."

"What does it even matter?" Becca demanded. "You're all made-up anyway."

I touched her arm in warning, but she jerked away.

"Sadie is a weak alter, and it would upset her to know about me. I am strong, and it's my job to keep the rest of them safe."

Zach had kept himself hidden, not only from all of us, but from Sadie, too, because he considered himself some sort of guardian. Only he wasn't trying to protect them from any real danger, but from the truth itself.

"And what about Millie?" I asked. "She couldn't even speak to tell Sadie the truth about her diagnosis."

"Millie spent her time sneaking around, and one night, she ended up in the wrong place at the wrong time."

"That day in the cafeteria when Sadie was yelling at Millie," Danny said, and I turned back to look at him. "She must have seen something."

Zach's expression darkened. "She interrupted my attempt to kill Jon."

Danny made a choking sound. "Why?"

"He relentlessly made fun of Sadie. She even tried to warn him, but he was too stupid to listen. He deserved to die."

So even emotional distress counted as something Zach needed to protect Sadie from. His explanations for why he killed revealed a highly distorted thinking process. In short, Zach was psychotic.

"That's insane!" Danny cried, and Zach jerked his head in Danny's direction and glared.

"What happened when Millie interrupted you?" I asked to distract him.

"I grabbed hold of her and said if she ever told anyone, she was next. I never got another opportunity to go to the boy's hallway again, but I would have gone first chance I had."

Before Danny could react again, I jumped in with another question. "What made you kill Millie?"

"She talked."

Becca sucked in her breath. To Zach, it was as simple as that. It didn't matter that Millie only said a few words. There was still the possibility that she could tell everyone that Sadie/Zach attempted to kill Jon. In my office, I had tried to get her to tell me about the confrontation with Sadie. Even then, I had been concerned. But I never could have guessed this.

The lack of remorse made it sound like this alter had the personality of a sociopath.

A murderous alter had been hiding inside Emma this whole time. When Emma first came here, her report read that the authorities suspected she had started the fire that burned her house down with her family inside. However, because of her non-violent history, I believed she had started it by accident. An arson investigation had been conducted, but when it came time to question Emma, she had already hidden away behind her alter, Lisa. The authorities had been unable to determine who had started the fire, and with Emma basically hidden away in a mental hospital, they never found the perpetrator. Now I knew Zach had been the one responsible. Despite all the safety measures in place in our facility, he had still managed to kill.

When we first found Katelyn, we thought she had overdosed somehow. That maybe she had been cheeking her pills, saving them up, and then took them all at one time. It had been devastating to hear that a patient killed herself on my watch. We went to great lengths to make our patients believe they didn't have access to anything dangerous—like glass or razors. My greatest fear was that other patients would figure out how to overdose after hearing about

Katelyn, so I had the staff spread the rumor that she had hanged herself. I did this because the light fixtures weren't strong enough to hold that much weight. Therefore, if any patients tried to commit suicide in the same way, they wouldn't succeed.

Because Katelyn had died at this facility, an investigation was conducted by the authorities. When I received her autopsy results, I had choked on my coffee. She had died from suffocation, not an overdose.

"Did you kill Emma's family, too?"

The change that overcame Emma's face chilled me. The alter's lips peeled back in a terrible grimace. "Someone had to."

This time, Aaron asked why.

"Emma's dad started sexually abusing her at the age of seven. He continued it nearly every day of her life until the day before I killed him. Never once did that bastard touch her sister, Amber. And instead of being a good older sister who protected Emma, Amber always treated her like a freak.

"Their mother loved Amber best, and maybe if she was the one he'd abused she would have done something about it. But it was Emma, so she turned a blind eye. This would have gone on forever if it hadn't been for me."

"Now Emma is orphaned without any family left," I said to gauge the reaction. "How is that better?"

"They deserved to die."

"That wasn't your decision to make. It only adds to the trauma that Emma must face."

"We won't let Emma feel any pain," Zach said with a haughty look.

"Then she won't ever recover," I said. "She'll always be a prisoner to her trauma. You can't live her life for her. Let her come out, and I will help her."

"You want to kill her!" Zach snarled. His hand tightened on the knife.

Sweat beaded along my hairline, and I resisted the urge to wipe it away. "That's your reaction to problems—not mine. I want to help her."

"Like you helped her before? Holding her down and drugging her? Locking her in a padded room?"

"That was for her safety."

Zach began to pace, and I touched the handle of my gun.

"Bullshit! You wanted to control her."

I had to remain calm. The other kids were counting on me to talk Zach down. "If you truly care about her, Zach, you'll let her go. We all have to face our own trauma. You can't protect her forever."

"I'm the *only* one who cares about her," he said in an ominous tone.

"Zach," I said, taking a step toward him and gesturing for the other patients to move farther behind me, "if you continue to control Emma, then my only choice will be to medically restrain her and put her in the padded room again. You are unstable and a murderer. We can't let you have free rein." He appeared to listen, and for a moment, my hopes lifted. "Please, let her go."

And then Zach's expression slammed closed. "Never."

With a yell, he launched Emma at us, knife held high.

Before I could stop him, Aaron ran forward to intercept her. She stabbed deeply into his shoulder and shoved him aside, pulling out a bloody knife. Aaron shouted in pain.

Emma barreled toward us, a grim determination on her plain face.

I had no choice. I sighted my gun and fired.

25

Dr. Williams

One week later, I sat at my desk and rubbed a hand over my face. A headache pounded at the base of my skull. Official letters from local law enforcement, the Georgia Medical Board, and bereaved families covered the surface. With a sigh, I got up and went over to my filing cabinet. Before I opened the drawer, I glanced up at the framed articles that had once given me so much pride. Now, I would only be remembered for how badly I let this situation get out of control.

I pulled out the most challenging case file I've ever had. The file folder bulged now from all the extra entries. I flipped to the beginning, three months ago when Emma Bryce first arrived at my facility.

ROLLING GREEN PEDIATRIC MENTAL HEALTH FACILITY

Intake Assessment

Name: Emma Bryce
Date of Birth: 8/07/2005
Client Identification Number: 35-6437

REASON FOR REFERRAL

Emma Bryce was ordered by the court to receive at least one year of mental health treatment at this facility, under the care of Dr. Williams. Although the case is still ongoing, it is believed Emma is responsible for the deaths of her parents and sister. When their house burned down two weeks ago, Emma was the sole survivor.

Emma has very little memory of the events of that night. She was catatonic when the paramedics arrived. This was believed to be due to shock. She later revived but still seemed to be trapped in a dissociative state, with long periods of silence and blank stares. She couldn't recall her name or birthdate. Later, she told the doctor examining her that her name was Lisa.

When I first read over her case file, I had been working under the assumption that Emma had been suffering from a temporary psychotic break that led to her burning down her childhood home. Emma's alter Lisa was not aggressive in any way. She tended to be overly anxious and fearful. Because of these traits, I wrongfully believed the psychotic symptoms had gone into remission. And although Sadie seemed a little more withdrawn and unwilling to open up during therapy, she hadn't displayed any signs of aggression either. Of course, I hadn't seen the truth until two of my patients had been killed. The real perpetrator had been hiding behind them the whole time.

Significant Personal Relationships

With her parents and sister deceased, Emma's only living relative is a paternal aunt. When we contacted her aunt about fostering Emma, she said, "I can't stand my brother or his family, and Emma has always creeped me out." Emma is therefore a ward of the state of Georgia.

It is suspected that Emma suffered abuse at the hands of one or both of her parents. Just the mention of her father produced an extreme reaction, where Emma immediately covered her ears, bent forward, and began rocking herself. She refused to explain what specifically upset her about her father, but she confessed that her mother clearly preferred her older sister. Both her parents and her sister frequently put her down verbally—calling her crazy, stupid, and worthless. Emma would often dissociate to avoid these attacks, as evidenced by saying she "blacked out" and "couldn't remember" what she did in response.

Her relationship with her sister Amber wasn't very unusual for two teenaged girls, but any sibling rivalry was exacerbated by their parents' favoritism toward Amber. As for friends, Emma seems sociable enough to make them, at least when she is dissociating as her alter Lisa, but she tends to keep them at a distance. Her anxiety, panic attacks, and frequent dissociating can also be draining on a relationship.

I frowned as I read over this section because I had always known Emma suffered from family trauma, but it wasn't until Zach told me about the sexual abuse that I knew for sure about Emma's father. The abuse acerbated the dissociating, and of course, it ended tragically for the whole family.

History of Present Illness

From past reports, Emma always had a strong imagination as a child. She preferred pretend play and imaginary friends over real life interaction. First diagnosed with sensory processing disorder and autism, this was later changed to dissociative identity disorder when Emma turned thirteen. By then, she had three distinct personalities:

Lisa: an anxious and fearful girl Emma's age who likes to perform well in school and spends a lot of time studying and reading.

Sadie: a girl who suffers from panic disorder but is generally less fearful than Lisa. She enjoys art and comic books and is skilled in making both.

Emma: main personality, rarely seen. Dissociates several times a day. Poor memory. Poor social skills.

I had added another entry below the others in the file now that we knew of his existence:

Zach: aggressive male personality type. Believes himself to be the "protector" of Emma and the other "weaker" personalities. Homicidal. Unrepentant. Murdered Emma's family. Confessed to the murders of Katelyn Alvirez and Millie Greene.

I reread the addition to the file, my mind still struggling with the idea that Emma's case was exceedingly rare. Not only was DID an unusual diagnosis—it affected less than two percent of the population in the entire world—but they were rarely the perpetrators of violence. Typically, patients with DID were the victims of violence, but Emma was both. I had two other patients with DID in my career as a psychiatrist, and neither had any violent tendencies. In fact, both had suffered from dissociation so profound they often became unresponsive. To have a more dominant and aggressive alter like Zach was almost unheard of, especially one who went as far as murder to protect his host.

I had plans to publish journal articles on Emma's symptoms. Others could learn from her case study and hopefully no one would make the same terrible mistake I did.

Current Symptoms

Emma arrived at the facility as the alternate personality Lisa. She had very little ability to recall what had happened to her family besides the fact that they died in a fire. She couldn't explain how she survived. We immediately began working on facing her trauma in order to reduce the need for the alternate personalities. Lisa was very resistant to treatment and would often end the session by covering her ears and screaming. After two months of working with her, the mention of her father and possible abuse caused Lisa to dissociate. She revived as a new alter: Sadie.

Sadie remembers less than Lisa and believes her parents are alive but her sister is dead. This could be to avoid discussing the past abuse of her father. Sadie suffers from anxiety, panic attacks, memory loss, nightmares, and delusions.

I wished I had realized the truth about what I thought were Sadie's delusions earlier. She believed her dreams were predictive of someone's death, and in a way, she was right. I just hadn't made the connection that the dreams were indicative of another, hidden alter.

Emma Bryce would be coming back to the mental facility today, having survived being shot. My jaw clenched as I closed my eyes against the onslaught of memories from the worst day of my career.

The day I had to shoot my own patient.

After she stabbed Aaron, I had aimed for a non-vital spot, but I was no marksman. Pulling the trigger had come with considerable risk. By some miracle, I hit her in the meaty part of her shoulder, which knocked her back powerfully. The shock of pain had been enough to make Zach lose his hold on her. Sadie had come through again, tears pouring from her eyes as she grabbed her shoulder protectively.

My stomach had twisted at the sight. The gun shook in my hand, but I didn't dare put it down. Knowing I had hurt my own patient tore me apart. However, I knew the gun was the only thing to keep the others safe. Emma's alter had already proven how dangerous he was, and I knew he wouldn't hesitate to hurt—and possibly even kill—them all.

Once I dealt with the much more docile Sadie, I retrieved a syringe of Haldol to subdue and sedate her until an ambulance could arrive. I gave her the injection and then helped her lie down on the floor to wait for the paramedics.

She didn't try to fight me when she saw the shot, just watched with huge, sorrowful eyes.

"I'm so sorry," she said. "I couldn't stop him from coming out. He was too strong."

"I know, Sadie. I'm sorry it all happened this way."

That was when she had noticed Aaron, lying on the floor. Her eyes had filled with tears. "No," she said. "Oh God, please tell me I didn't kill him."

The others had clustered around Aaron protectively, and both Becca and Danny showed signs of acute trauma. Their eyes were wide, tremors shook their bodies, and tears ran unchecked down their faces. The fact that I had failed to protect them from this weighed heavily on me.

"He's alive," Becca had said in her most matter-of-fact tone.

Sadie had let out her breath in relief. "I'm sorry, Aaron, I don't even know how to tell you . . ."

But he had turned his head away from her. The color drained from her face, and she bit her lip as though holding back a sob. The Haldol worked its magic then. Her limbs went slack as she slipped into unconsciousness.

Once she had succumbed to the effects of the sedative, I turned my attention to Aaron. He was sitting up—a good sign. Blood stained his scrubs all around the wound, and he covered it protectively with his other hand.

As I examined Aaron's knife wound, I would have done anything to go back in time and change this terrible outcome. I should have figured it out faster. I should have known that Emma's alter had been hiding a terrible secret.

Aaron had found out the truth too late.

The knife blade had cut deeply into the back of Aaron's left shoulder. As I gently probed the wound, Aaron gritted his teeth and groaned. I couldn't tell, of course, how much damage had been done to the muscles and tendons of the joint. But I could see from the way the blood wasn't massively pumping out of his body that at least she hadn't hit any major arteries.

I knew adrenaline and my medical training were the only things that had kept me from collapsing from exhaustion. If only I had paid closer attention to Emma's case, I might have arrived at the truth faster. Sadie had been accurate when she said I was only looking out for my reputation. At that thought, guilt wormed its way into my heart.

I had realized that night the whole situation would result in a criminal investigation of me, but I accepted that. I deserved it.

A knock rapped once on my door, drawing me out of my memories, and I rose to open it.

Aaron stood with his shoulder heavily bandaged but otherwise in good shape. He still wore his guarded expression, typical for Aaron. I suspected he had learned to hide his thoughts and feelings while in a gang. You didn't stay alive long if you revealed every emotion on your face.

"Aaron, please come and sit," I said, gesturing toward my old couch. "How are you?"

He hesitated for a moment, like he was considering just turning around and leaving instead. I tried not to take it personally. The kid had been through a lot. Aaron spent only a day in the hospital for his knife wound before returning here, but we didn't want to put him under too much mental stress by forcing him into group or individual therapy. I told him that he could decide when to see me to debrief what had happened.

Today was the first time he had reached out and asked for a meeting.

He sat down carefully, like he still had to protect his injury. "My shoulder feels better. It just gets really sore when PT works with me," he said, looking down at his hands.

Physical therapy was helping Aaron make sure he got full mobility back. "I'm glad to hear it. I don't want you to have lasting physical scars from all of this."

He shrugged with his good arm. "I still feel like a snitch for telling you about Sadie."

"You saved them all, Aaron. Zach would have gone on hurting people, and it would have taken us even longer to figure out what was going on."

I still thought about that moment, a couple hours before I ended up having to shoot Sadie. Aaron had come running to find me, his face taking on a grayish tint. "I think Lisa—Sadie," he had corrected himself with a shake of his head. "I think Sadie might be responsible for Katelyn's and Millie's deaths, and she is about to discover the truth about herself. I'm afraid of what she'll do then. She thinks they didn't', and I think she suspects you," he told me.

I had looked at him with surprise. I never would have thought Sadie blamed me for their deaths. "What makes her think that?" I had asked Aaron.

"She told us about how Katelyn and Millie both

went into your office and came out crying before they died. She planned to break into your office and go through your stuff to see if she could find anything incriminating. I was going to help, too," he said with a shake of his head. "But then she mentioned Lisa—like she thinks Lisa was killed, too, and then I knew she'd totally lost it."

Nurse Denise had called me and filled me in on the chaos happening at the facility, and luckily, I didn't live far away. She told me about finding Sadie snooping in my office, but she didn't know the motive behind it. Judging by the mess the techs had been forced to clean up, she suspected other patients were involved, but she didn't know who yet. Aaron had been the one to seek her out and tell her Sadie was in my office going through the file cabinets. Nurse Denise had immediately taken Sadie to isolation where she would be safe until I could examine her, but Aaron had waited to explain to me why she would do such a thing.

"Sadie's safe in isolation, Aaron," I had said.

"Not anymore. I saw them all running down the hall."

I froze. "Who helped her get out?" I had demanded.

"Becca swiped the keys in the nurse's station. Danny and Jon are helping her, though."

My chest had tightened at the news. I didn't want other patients involved in this. It was too dangerous. Unfortunately, Becca, Danny, and Jon had completely bought into Sadie's story. They knew something was off about Katelyn's and Millie's deaths, and they had been right. They just had the wrong suspect in mind. That was when I'd reached into my drawer and retrieved my gun.

"You did the right thing, Aaron," I said. "Now I need you to go back to your room where it's safe."

He had said he would and believing him was my mistake. Instead of doing as I asked, he had followed me without my knowing. He jumped out just as I intercepted Sadie and the others.

I had asked Nurse Denise and the two techs on night shift to try and find Sadie and the others if they could, but they also needed to make sure the rest of the patients stayed safely in their rooms. With a skeleton staff, we didn't have enough manpower to do everything at once. I regretted that, too, because it ended up getting Aaron stabbed and Jon knocked unconscious.

"How are you and Jon after all this?" I asked him now.

"Better. He forgave me for knocking him out, and I decided to let it go that he attacked me in the first place. We were both misled."

"I'm glad to hear it. There's always the option to change roommates if needed."

He shook his head. "It's fine."

When he fell silent, I leaned forward to tell him what I had been thinking about since all this started. "I owe you an apology, Aaron, for everything that happened. Not only your injury, but the fact that you got caught up in another patient's delusion. I should have been more diligent. I didn't realize you had developed such a strong relationship with Lisa."

He hung his head. "I feel like an idiot now."

"Please don't. That's the last thing I want you to feel. Alters can be extremely convincing as authentic people. The fact is, none of us have communicated with Emma Bryce since her family burned in that fire. From the moment she was picked up by paramedics and taken to the hospital, she identified herself as Lisa. As you can imagine, it caused a lot of confusion and mix-ups for the medical staff."

"But I shouldn't have gotten involved with Sadie, too. I knew it, but it was like I couldn't stay away. I just felt like I had this connection to Lisa, and obviously Sadie looked just like her."

"Of course. And I made a mistake telling all of you to treat Sadie as a new patient and not tell her the truth about Lisa. My thinking at the time was that bringing up Lisa could cause her to dissociate, which would further delay her progress."

I had worked with Emma from the beginning on addressing the trauma that caused her to protect her mind by dissociating. The dissociation caused the alters. The trouble was, I didn't realize she had any alters besides Lisa. The closer we got to the truth of Emma's trauma, the more unstable Lisa became. It got to the point where she would come to my office and sit in silence, staring out the window and refusing to answer questions beyond a simple yes or no. Eventually, I pushed too hard, and Lisa disappeared. Next I knew, Sadie believed she had just arrived at the mental facility.

"There is one thing I wanted to ask you about," Aaron said, and I braced myself. I had made what I considered a laundry list of mistakes, and it made my muscles twitch to hear them pointed out.

"Anything I can answer, I will."

"Sadie said that Katelyn and Millie were both really upset after being in your office for hours right before they died. What happened?"

I frowned, the memories of pushing them too

hard in therapy taking hold of me. In hindsight, it seemed to be a common theme with me. When I got frustrated by a patient's lack of progress, I became impatient and refused to give them time to open up on their own. "Sadie told me that Katelyn mentioned Lisa to her, so I called Katelyn in to see me and reminded her how important it was not to talk about Emma's alters. I scolded Katelyn too hard for it, which upset her. I shouldn't have come on so strong, but all I could think about was it potentially hindering the progress I had made with Sadie."

Aaron nodded like he had already suspected that to be the case. "And Millie?"

I pulled my glasses off so I could rub my face. "Millie is another case of a patient I pushed too hard. I was just so encouraged by the fact that she had spoken her first words in many years. I wanted to capitalize on that and hopefully get her to reveal more about her past. Millie had suffered a terribly traumatic childhood, but no one has ever known exactly what caused her to stop speaking. I thought I could finally get her to tell me the truth. But the mention of her past shut her down and upset her terribly. I spent hours trying to calm her after that." I didn't tell him the rest. That my own hubris had made me push her. I had looked at my ridiculous framed articles and imagined new ones touting my success on curing a patient with selective mutism.

Aaron stayed quiet for a moment. "And then the next day, she was dead. Because of Sadie. Well, Zach, I guess."

I nodded. "Yes, but I now believe Sadie had inklings of this alter's activities through her dreams."

"She did mention having dreams about Katelyn and Millie dying. She thought she was psychic. I never would have guessed she was actually the killer," he said, looking sick.

"No one knew about the other alter," I said. "It was your quick thinking that helped me catch her and stop her from harming anyone else. And for that, I think your time here is nearly at an end. I plan to discharge you in four weeks instead of eight."

He closed his eyes in what looked like relief. "Does the judge know?"

"Yes, I've already written to him that I'm recommending an early release."

"Thank you, Dr. Williams."

"Of course. Is there anything else you wanted to talk about today?"

He shook his head and stood. "No, I don't really want to get into any emotional therapy stuff right now."

"I understand. But Aaron, you've been through a lot. Before you leave, we'll have to talk about the impact it had on you, all right?"

"Fine," he said and turned for the door. Before he could reach it though, he stopped. "What about Sadie?"

"What about her?"

"Is she still at the hospital?"

"She's being released today and is in transit back here."

He looked thoughtful. "Will it be Sadie again?"

"I don't know. I have high hopes of finally being able to talk to Emma."

"Well," he said, jaw tightening, "whoever she is, keep her the hell away from me."

On that note, he left. I couldn't blame him. I wouldn't want anything to do with her if I was Aaron either. But I was her psychiatrist, and at one time, I used to be a damn good one, so I wouldn't give up on her.

I watched out my office window while the transport vehicle drove around the circular driveway with Emma Bryce inside. The brief winter in Georgia had already lost its hold, and I noticed little green shoots peeking through the pine straw in the flower beds. The dogwood tree in the center of the driveway already had green buds. Spring would be here soon.

The seasons affected the patients' moods, and an increase in sunshine, daffodils blooming, and warmer weather would help many of them cross that last hurdle, putting their illnesses into regression.

Whether it worked for someone as severe as Emma, though, remained to be seen.

As she exited the van, I watched her movements closely. Too well, I remembered how she looked when Zach had been in control. But now, my heart felt a little lighter. She stepped out cautiously, her gaze darting across the landscape. There was no aggressive posturing or masculine stature. For just a moment, she tilted her freckled face to the sunshine and closed her eyes.

I knew then that there was hope.

Christine, one of the nurses, met her at the front entrance. Emma followed her meekly.

I turned back to my desk and prepared my notepad and pen. Christine would bring her straight here, and I would evaluate her for the third time.

I chewed the end of my pen, something I hadn't done since I was in med school, overwhelmed by my studies.

No matter who walked through that door, I would peel through the layers to get to Emma. She was in there somewhere.

A soft knock came, and then Christine opened the door. "I have your next patient to see you," she said, and my stomach churned as Emma walked through the door, arm in a sling.

I stood and came out from behind my desk. As I smiled and held my hand out for her to sit on the couch, Christine left, shutting the door quietly behind her.

"Hello," I said. "I'm Dr. Williams."

Emma smiled shyly. "Vanessa."

My heart thudded in my chest. Another alter we had never encountered before. But was Vanessa more like Sadie, or more like Zach?

Only one way to find out.

"So tell me, Vanessa. Why do you think you're here?"

Thank you for reading I KNOW YOU KILLED THEM! If you enjoyed the book, we would greatly appreciate it if you could consider adding a review on your bookstore of choice.

Reviews make a huge difference to the success or failure of a book, especially for writers like us. The more reviews a book has, the more people are likely to take a shot on picking it up. The review need only be a line or two, and it really would make the world of difference for us if you could spare the three minutes it takes to leave one.

With all our thanks,

J.A. Leake & Jack McSporran

www.ingramcontent.com/pod-product-compliance
Lightning Source LLC
Chambersburg PA
CBHW021219220726
48287CB00015B/1698